GORE VIDAL wrote his first novel, *W[...]* while overseas in World War II. Du[...] has written novels, plays, short sto[...] political activist. As a Democratic c[...] New York, he received the most vot[...] From 1970 to 1972 he was co-ch[...] the People's Party. In California's 1982 Democratic primary for U.S. Senate, he polled a half-million votes, and came in second in a field of nine.

In 1948 Vidal wrote the highly praised international best-seller *The City and the Pillar*. This was followed by *The Judgment of Paris* and the prophetic *Messiah*. In the fifties Vidal wrote plays for live television and films for Metro-Goldwyn-Mayer. One of the television plays became the successful Broadway play *Visit to a Small Planet* (1957). Directly for the theater he wrote the prize-winning hit *The Best Man* (1960). In 1964 Vidal returned to the novel with *Julian*, the story of the apostate Roman emperor. This novel has been published in many languages and editions. As Henry de Montherlant wrote: "*Julian* is the only book about a Roman emperor that I like to re-read. Vidal loves his protagonist; he knows the period thoroughly; and the book is a beautiful hymn to the twilight of paganism." During the last quarter-century Vidal has been telling the history of the United States as experienced by one family and its connections in what Gabriel García Márquez has called "Gore Vidal's magnificent series of historical novels or novelized histories." They are, in chronological order, *Burr, Lincoln, 1876, Empire, Hollywood, Washington, D.C.* and *The Golden Age*.

During the same period, Vidal invented a series of satiric comedies – *Myra Breckinridge, Myron, Kalki, Duluth*. "Vidal's development . . . along that line from *Myra Breckinridge* to *Duluth* is crowned with success," wrote Italo Calvino in *La Repubblica* (Rome). "I consider Vidal to be a master of that new form which is taking shape in world literature and which we may call the hyper-novel or the novel elevated to the square or to the cube." To this list Vidal added the highly praised – and controversial – *Live from Golgotha* in 1992. *Palimpsest*, his highly acclaimed memoir, was published in 1995 and was followed by *The Smithsonian Institution,* published in 1998. The collection of his works – *The Essential Gore Vidal* – was published in 1999.

Vidal has also published several volumes of essays. When the National Book Critics Circle presented him with an award (1982), the citation read: "The American tradition of independent and curious learning is kept alive in the wit and great expressiveness of Gore Vidal's criticism." In 1993, he won the National Book Award for *United States: Essays 1952–1992*.

Vidal co-starred with Tim Robbins in the movie *Bob Roberts*.

Books by Gore Vidal

NOVELS

Narratives of Empire
Burr
Lincoln
1876
Empire
Hollywood
Washington, D.C.
The Golden Age

Williwaw
In a Yellow Wood
The City and the Pillar
The Season of Comfort
A Search for the King
Dark Green, Bright Red
The Judgment of Paris
Messiah
Julian
Myra Breckinridge
Two Sisters
Myron
Kalki
Creation
Duluth
Live from Golgotha
The Smithsonian Institution

MEMOIR

Palimpsest: A Memoir
Point to Point Navigation

SHORT STORIES

A Thirsty Evil

PLAYS

An Evening with Richard Nixon
Weekend
Romulus
The Best Man
Visit to a Small Planet

NON-FICTION

Rocking the Boat
Reflections upon a Sinking Ship
Homage to Daniel Shays
Matters of Fact and of Fiction
Pink Triangle and Yellow Star
Armageddon?
At Home
Screening History
A View from the Diners Club
United States: Essays 1952–1992
Virgin Islands
The Essential Gore Vidal
The Last Empire

IN A YELLOW WOOD

Gore Vidal

ABACUS

First published in Great Britain in 1967 by the New English Library Limited
Reissued in 1979 by William Heinemann
Published in 1980 by Granada Publishing Limited in Panther Books
This edition published by Abacus in 2005
Reprinted 2009

A CIP catalogue record for this book
is available from the British Library.

ISBN 978-0-349-11699-0

Printed and bound in Great Britain by Clays Ltd, St Ives plc

Papers used by Abacus are natural, renewable and recyclable
products sourced from well-managed forests and certified
in accordance with the rules of the Forest Stewardship Council.

Mixed Sources
Product group from well-managed
forests and other controlled sources
www.fsc.org   Cert no. SGS-COC-004081
© 1996 Forest Stewardship Council
FSC

Abacus
An imprint of
Little, Brown Book Group
100 Victoria Embankment
London EC4Y 0DY

An Hachette UK Company
www.hachette.co.uk

www.littlebrown.co.uk

For Anais Nin

1
DAY

Two roads diverged in a yellow wood,
And sorry I could not travel both
And be one traveller ...

— FROST

ONE

Robert Holton removed several dark hairs from his comb and wondered if his hairline was receding. He squinted for a moment at himself in the mirror and decided that he was not losing his hair, not yet anyway.

Then he sat down on the edge of the bed and put on his shoes. He started to tie the laces of the left shoe when he began to think of his dream. He had many dreams: of flying through the air, of walking in empty rooms, of all the standard things that psychiatrists like to hear about. Unfortunately, in the morning he could seldom recall what he had dreamed the night before. He would remember the sensation of the dream but nothing else. He would remember if it had been good or bad but that was all. Last night his dream had been unpleasant and something in the room had suddenly recalled it to him.

Robert Holton frowned and tried to remember. Was it the carpet? He had looked at the carpet while tying his shoe. He looked at it now. The carpet was dusty and uninteresting. It was a solid brown colour; the same carpet that covered the floor of every hotel room in New York. No, the carpet was not connected with his dream.

He had been standing at the dresser while combing his hair. He looked at the dresser; plain dull wood with dull scrollwork about the mirror. On the dresser was a dingy white cloth and on the cloth were a pair of brushes, his wallet, and a collection of small things. Nothing suggested an unpleasant dream.

The morning light glowed yellowly through the window shade. There was a band of brighter light between the bottom

3

of the shade and the window sill and here the daylight shone into the square room where Robert Holton lived. He looked at the sunlight a moment and forgot his dream.

He glanced at his watch : fifteen minutes to eight. He had to be at the office at eight-thirty. Quickly he tied his shoes and got to his feet. He searched through the bureau drawers for a shirt. He found a white one and put it on. Before the war he had worn coloured shirts but now plain white ones seemed more sound. And then it was a good idea not to be too vivid when you worked for a brokerage house.

His tie was pretty, though. It was a striped one, blue and white. Not a dark sullen blue but a light and casual blue. As he knotted his tie in front of the mirror he noticed his face was pale. He was always pale in the morning, of course; still, he looked unhealthy in the city. This morning he looked paler than usual. There were no pouches under his eyes, though, and he was glad of that. Robert Holton looked younger than twenty-six. His features were boyish and undistinguished and certain women had said that he was handsome. Robert Holton had looked well in uniform.

He put on his trousers and tightened the belt. Robert Holton, though he had never been much of an athlete, had a good build. Sitting at desks, however, would ruin it sooner or later and the thought made him sad. There was nothing he could do, of course, for he would always sit at desks.

He picked up his coat from the chair where he had hung it the night before and put it on. He posed for a moment in front of the mirror. Perhaps he was not handsome but he was nicer looking than a great many people and it is better to be nicer looking than a great many people than to be unusually handsome.

Robert Holton turned from the window and went into the bathroom. His watch was on the tile floor beside the bath-tub where he had left it the night before. He set the watch by his alarm clock.

Again he tried to recall his dream. On the wall there was a picture of some apples on a table. A Frenchman had painted the picture twenty years before. It had been re-produced and the hotel had bought several copies because

4

they were cheap and because the manager's wife had thought the picture pleasant. Robert Holton liked the picture. It seemed to suggest his dream to him more than anything else in the room. He studied the picture but he could not remember the dream. The picture only made him uneasy. He looked away.

He went to the closet and took out his trench coat. He had bought it when he became a lieutenant three years before.

It was almost eight o'clock now. Robert Holton opened the door of his room and stepped out into the corridor.

There was a difference in smell. The corridor smelled old and dusty as though no one had walked down it in years. Robert Holton in the one year he had lived in this hotel had never seen anyone else come out of a room. Sometimes he wondered if he might not be the only person living on this floor, or in this hotel, or in the world.

The ceiling of the corridor was high and he enjoyed walking under such a high ceiling. He walked to the elevator and pressed the button marked 'Down'.

There was a large pot filled with white sand beside the elevator door. He had always wanted to put something into that white sand. A cigarette butt, anything at all to spoil the white smooth surface. One day he would spit on the sand; he made himself that promise.

There was a clatter as the elevator went past his floor. That always happened. He pushed the button angrily.

Robert Holton tried to recall what he was supposed to do that day at the office. He could think of nothing very important that had to be done. In the afternoon he was supposed to go to a cocktail party and he looked forward to that. Mrs Raymond Stevanson was giving it and she was a very proper person to know. She had been a friend of his mother's and she had been nice to Robert Holton when his mother had died several years earlier. His father thought Mrs Raymond Stevanson was stupid but his father was often harsh and she was, after all, important socially. When one was starting out in the brokerage business contacts were important. He began to map his day in detail.

There was a loud rattling and the elevator stopped at his

5

floor. The door opened and Robert Holton stepped into the elevator.

'Good morning, Mr Holton,' said the elevator boy, a young man in his middle teens.

'Good morning, Joe. What kind of a day is it?'

'Wonderful out. Real warm for this time of year. Real Indian summer outside. Real nice weather.'

'That's fine,' said Robert Holton, glad to hear that the weather was good.

'Any news on the market?' asked Joe, stopping at the seventh floor.

'Nothing new.' A middle-aged man, tall and thin, came into the elevator. Robert Holton had seen him almost every day for a year but they never spoke. The middle-aged man wore a black shiny topcoat and he carried a large leather brief case in which the outlines of an apple could be seen.

'I guess there's nothing for me to put my money in, I guess,' said Joe.

'I shouldn't advise buying now,' said Robert Holton. 'It was a daily joke of theirs. Joe would pretend he had money to invest and wanted advice.

They stopped at the second floor and another tall thin man in a shiny overcoat got into the elevator. This man had a red face, though, and the other man had a white face. Neither of them ever spoke. Robert Holton often wondered what they did for a living, whether they had wives or not.

'Well, here we are,' said Joe, opening the door. 'We made it all right this time.'

'We certainly did.' Robert Holton followed the two older men out of the elevator and into the lobby.

The lobby was high-ceilinged and old-fashioned. Tropical bushes grew in buckets and a grey chandelier was suspended from the centre of the ceiling. At the desk sat a faded little woman.

She nodded to Robert Holton and he nodded to her. They never spoke. He picked up a newspaper from the desk, looked at his mail box to see if he might have overlooked something the night before. Finding nothing, he put three cents in a saucer beside the newspapers.

6

Robert Holton went outside. The morning was clear and cool. There was a depth, a golden depth in the air. There was no time of the year as pleasant as autumn, thought Robert Holton; unless it was spring. He liked spring, too.

He walked down the not yet busy side street where he lived. His footsteps sounded sharp and loud on the pavement. The brownstone houses that lined the street seemed large and significant this morning. Perhaps it was because of the clearness of the day. He noticed details in the stone that he had never noticed before. For instance, one of the houses was built of oddly pitted stone. He had seen another place built of pitted stone. He thought a moment : Notre Dame, the cathedral in Paris. During the war he had seen it. He had even walked up a great many winding steps to get to the top. At the top he had noticed the pitted stone which had proved, somehow or other, that the building was very old.

Sleepy children were coming out of the houses. They walked down the street to the bus stop, schoolbooks under their arms. There was a smell of bacon and coffee in the air and Robert Holton's stomach contracted hungrily.

At the end of the street was the subway station. Every morning he disappeared down it and every evening he came up out of it. He spent a lot of time in the subway.

He went down the dirty cement steps. He put a nickel into the turnstile and walked out on to the cement platform. Twenty or thirty men and women stood on the platform with him, waiting for the downtown train.

The express went crashing by them. The noise of these trains was terrific. After it had passed he had to yawn several times to clear the deafness from his ears. Then the local stopped and he got aboard.

He sat next to a stout man who lived in his hotel. Occasionally they would speak.

'How's the market?' asked the fat man, deciding not to read his paper.

'The market's doing fine, should go up.'

'Well, that sure is good news. I've a little bit that I'd like to put in it. I'd like to put it in something safe, though. You

7

know of something safe? Something that's going to go way up, say?'

'Well, that's a hard question. It's very hard to tell just yet. Sugar's doing well,' said Robert Holton. He always said the same things to these questions. No one cared what he said. They would repeat it to acquaintances, saying that a friend of theirs in Wall Street had advised them to buy sugar but they didn't feel it was such a good buy at this time.

'You was in the army, weren't you?' asked the stout man suddenly.

Robert Holton nodded.

'Been out long?'

'Over a year.'

'I'll bet you was glad to get out. To get away from all those rules and things, those restrictions. I was in the army in the last war. I guess the one before last, you'd call it now. I was sure glad to get out.'

'Everyone is,' said Robert Holton and he thought of the things that he had done in London. He had liked London.

'You went to college, didn't you?' asked the stout man; he was trying to clear up something in his mind.

'That's right.'

'That's what I thought. Me, I never had the opportunity. I had to go to work,' said the stout man with pride. 'I had to work when I was a youngster. I never went to college.'

'It's a good experience,' said Robert Holton, wishing the man would read his paper and stop asking questions. The train went around a corner noisily; blue electric sparks sparkled outside the window. Then the train straightened out again.

'I'm in the grocery business,' said the stout man.

'I know,' said Robert Holton, 'we've talked about that before.'

'I started right in at the bottom,' said the stout man.

'That's the best place to start,' said Robert Holton, feeling that there was no answer to this. He was wrong.

'Well, I don't know. It's hard to say. How *did* you like the army?'

'It wasn't bad.'

8

'It wasn't good either. I never got overseas last time, I mean time before last, but we had it rough in training.'

'I can imagine.' Robert Holton looked away and the stout man stopped talking. Robert Holton looked at the upper moulding of the car to see if there were any new advertisements. There weren't any. His special favourite, a girl advertising beer, was behind him and he couldn't see it. Gloomily he examined a fat red child devouring a piece of bread. This was the advertisement he liked least. He looked away.

A woman with a small child sat across from him, directly under the bread advertisement. The woman was heavy with a roll of flesh around her middle; she wore a tight black dress. The child with her was about the age of the one in the picture. This child was pale, though, pale and fat.

A Negro was asleep next to the woman and child. He was long and thin and his bare ankles and wrists looked like brown wood. Two Jewish secretaries with yellow hair talked brightly together. They were young women and wore gaily coloured clothes and their plump legs were hairless and pink.

An old woman with grey hair and deep lines in her face looked at the two young women and seemed to hate them in a secret womanly manner. Several young boys, wearing discarded army clothing, sat in a corner, their schoolbooks beside them. They talked in hoarse changing voices. Robert Holton could not hear what they were saying but their voices seemed to speak of sexual things.

The train stopped at a station and the stout man left. Two more stops and Robert Holton would get off.

The car was beginning to empty. Only the two girls were opposite him. They still talked brightly and laughed too loudly, conscious that he was watching them.

The train made its two stops and the girls got off. No one sat opposite him now. He studied the advertisements.

Then his stop was made. Quickly he got up, his trench coat under his arm. He went out on to the platform and before the train left he looked in again through the window. Slightly to the right of where he had been sitting was the

9

picture of the girl advertising beer. He looked at her until the
train pulled out.

When the train was gone he turned and walked up the
dirty cement steps and as he walked he wished that he had
a girl as pretty as the one who advertised beer.

TWO

'Hurry up, Marjorie. Let's get those tables cleaned up.'

'Yes,' said Marjorie Ventusa, 'yes, Mrs Merrin, I certainly will,' she spoke sweetly, hoping that Mrs Merrin would get the sarcasm in her voice, but Mrs Merrin was already at the other end of the restaurant talking to another waitress.

Marjorie pushed her natural blonde hair out of her eyes. She was never able to keep it in order; perhaps she should have it cut shorter, wear a snood perhaps. Mrs Merrin was watching her, she noticed. Quickly Marjorie began to put the dirty dishes on her tray.

People were coming in and out of the restaurant. It got a lot of the less wealthy Wall Street trade. Clerks and secretaries and stenographers had breakfast and lunch here and the lonelier ones had supper here. When her tray was full she went back to the kitchen.

On the other side of the swinging doors the cooks, wearing fairly clean aprons and white hats, were cooking at ranges. There was always steam and the smell of soap in the air. People shouted at one another and it was like a war. Marjorie hated the kitchen. The front part of the restaurant was all right. She had been a waitress off and on for fifteen years and she didn't mind noisy people and the clattering of dishes.

She put some glasses of water on her tray before she left the kitchen. Then Marjorie Ventusa gave the swinging door a kick and walked back into the dining room. She had five tables to take care of.

Two women were seated at the table she had just cleared. She could tell from the backs of their heads that they were secretaries and older women; this meant they would be very particular and leave a ten-cent tip for both of them.

'Good morning,' said Marjorie Ventusa, smiling brightly and thinking of nothing at all. She put the water glasses on the table. The two women were frowning at their menus.

'How much extra is a large orange juice?' asked one.

'It's ten cents more if you take it with the breakfast.'

'All right, I'll take a double orange juice, some toast and coffee. Do you have any marmalade?'

'Yes, ma'am.'

'Well, bring some of that, too.'

The other woman said, 'The same for me.' Marjorie Ventusa picked up their menus. As she was turning to go she saw Robert Holton come into the restaurant and she was suddenly happy. She smiled at him and he, seeing her, smiled back. She pointed to one of her tables and he sat down at it. Quickly she went back to the kitchen to give her orders. She pushed her hair back from her face and promised herself that she would get a snood the next day.

Marjorie Ventusa liked Robert Holton. For a year he had been coming into the restaurant; he always spoke pleasantly to her and they would joke together. She had never seen him anywhere except in the restaurant. She knew that he never really noticed her but she was always glad to see him and she was delighted when he talked to her and smiled at her; his smile was pleasant and he had nice teeth. She thought him handsome.

'Good morning, Mr Holton,' she said, putting a glass of water and some silverware on his table.

'How're you today, Marjorie? You look perfect.'

'Sure, sure, I do; I'm a real beauty.' Marjorie always felt awkward with him, as though she couldn't think of the right words to say. She was older than he was, too. Marjorie was thirty-seven; she had known a lot of men and still she was awkward with him.

'What you going to have this morning?' she asked.

'Well . . .' He drawled the word as he looked at the menu and she had a strong urge to touch the short dark hairs on the back of his neck. She tried to think of some excuse to do

12

so. Then she was angry with herself for having thought of such a thing.

'I guess I'll have some orange juice and scrambled eggs and bacon.'

'Is that all you going to eat? Why, how you ever going to get big and strong?'

He laughed. 'Not sitting at a desk and eating your cooking.'

'Oh, is that so?' Marjorie Ventusa walked slowly back to the kitchen. She felt strained as she walked for she could feel he was watching her. She wished suddenly that her hips weren't so big and that her legs were slimmer.

She shouted his order to the cooks, then she took the two secretaries' breakfasts out to them. They complained bitterly about the size of the orange juice and one said that it was too sour and the other said that there were seeds in it.

'I'm sorry,' said Marjorie, 'would you like something else?'

They said they would not and acted as if she had grown the oranges badly and had put seeds in the juice. One of her other tables was full now and she went and took their order.

Out in the kitchen his breakfast was ready and she put it on her tray. There were some seeds in the orange juice which she carefully removed with a spoon.

He was reading his paper when she came back. He didn't look up as she arranged the dishes on his table.

'Well, here's your breakfast,' she said. 'You better eat it while it's hot.'

'Oh, sure.' Robert Holton folded his paper and laid it on the table. She watched him as he drank the orange juice.

'Sour, isn't it?' she asked.

'A little bit, maybe.'

'I'm glad you're not going to complain. The rest, they all complain all the time. I get so tired sometimes I could get sick; I get so tired of listening to them.'

'Just don't take them seriously. Everybody feels awful in the morning. You've just been awake longer and you feel better than they do, that's all.'

Marjorie Ventusa laughed admiringly. 'I wouldn't have

ever thought of that,' she said. 'You might be right. Anyway a girl gets pretty tired of being shouted at all the time like it's her fault.'

'Well, just relax. I like the food and the service.'

'Thank you,' she said, trying to sound elegant and funny at the same time.

'When you going to go out dancing with me?' Robert Holton asked, sawing a piece of bacon in half with a blunt knife.

'I'm pretty busy,' she said; she always said that when he asked her that question. He would say it because he thought it was funny and she would answer him as though she thought it was funny too. She wished that he meant it now. She had always wished that he meant it. 'I'm pretty busy,' she said. 'I got so many people asking to go out with me. You'd have to wait a couple of weeks, maybe.'

'I can wait,' he said, smiling at her; smiling the way he would to a child, she thought suddenly. She watched him eat.

'Marjorie,' said a voice behind her.

'Yes, Mrs Merrin, I'm coming. I'll be right with you. I was just cleaning this table."

Mrs Merrin was tall and stout with a wide loose mouth which she could make look stern and harsh when she wanted to. She made it look that way now.

'Marjorie,' she said in a low voice, 'you stop your hanging around and talking to the customers. I tell you I won't stand for it.'

'I'm sorry, Mrs Merrin. I was just cleaning the table.' Mrs Merrin smiled warmly at Robert Holton and walked away.

'She's an awful bitch,' said Marjorie Ventusa.

'What did she say?' asked Robert Holton. 'I didn't hear her.'

'She was just running off at the mouth, that's all. She thought I was talking too much to you.'

One of her tables called for a check and she walked over quickly and put their used plates on her tray. Then she went back to the kitchen. More orders were ready for her. She loaded her tray and went back to work.

As she worked she watched Robert Holton. It was twenty

14

minutes past eight and she knew that he had to be at his office at eight-thirty. She hoped that he would stay as long as possible. His office was only a block away and he would be able to stay until eight-thirty. He ate slowly, she knew, and he would read his paper as he ate.

She hurried back to the kitchen. Two waitresses were talking and laughing together in a corner. They were young and pretty and would probably marry in another year and never work again; in another year Marjorie Ventusa would still be waiting on tables.

She stopped in front of the mirror behind the swinging door. Mrs Merrin always said that neatness was an important thing.

Marjorie Ventusa rubbed the kitchen steam from the mirror. Her hair was back in her face again. She pushed it viciously out of the eyes. She hated its colour. It was pale blonde, a real pale blonde. But because she was getting older and because she was part Italian everyone thought that she dyed her hair. She wondered if perhaps she shouldn't have it coloured black. Her eyebrows were dark, thin and dark, and that made the colour of her hair look even more suspicious.

A sailor she had seen several times during the war had told her that she had a beautiful figure and she had tried to believe him. She was too heavy, though. Well, she hadn't been heavy at that time. At least not quite so heavy as she was now. She wondered what kind of woman Robert Holton liked.

'Marjorie,' said Mrs Merrin. That was all Mrs Merrin said as she walked by. Marjorie Ventusa was glad. One day she would lose her temper and get fired.

The mirror had steamed up again. She took her tray and went out into the dining-room. More customers had come. She put glasses of water and silverware on their tables and took their orders and gave them instructions in how to order and how to avoid paying extra for what they wanted.

Robert Holton was halfway through his breakfast. She looked at the clock over the kitchen doors. It was twenty-seven minutes after eight o'clock. She would work very hard now to get her orders taken care of and then she would have a few minutes to talk to him before he left. She usually couldn't talk to him at lunch because he was always with someone else.

Marjorie Ventusa travelled quickly back and forth from kitchen to dining-room and back again. Her hair was hopelessly out of shape now and she was perspiring.

Finally her last customer was satisfied for the moment. She wandered casually over to Robert Holton's table.

'Breakfast good?' she asked.

'Never better.'

'That don't make it so good.' They laughed. He was always so polite with her. That was why she liked him, she thought. He was very kind. He was handsome, too, but that wasn't as important as being polite. A lot of fine people were not handsome.

'What's in the paper?' she asked. She never quite knew what to talk about when she was with him.

'Not much. The same old stuff. Election stuff mostly.'

'Seems like there's always an election.'

'There're a lot of them.'

'I almost don't read any newspapers. I don't seem to get time to read. I'll bet you read a lot of them.'

'I have to. I read all about the market.'

'That's right, you're in Wall Street. That must be exciting. Working there where all those big deals are made.'

'They don't make them where I am.' He laughed. 'I'm just another worker.'

'I thought you were way up in one of the big houses.'

'Well, sort of a clerk which doesn't pay much. It's a good way to starve.'

'You ought to do something different. Suppose you marry some girl ...'

'I'm not getting married for a long time.'

'I suppose,' said Marjorie Ventusa calmly, 'that you got some nice society girl all lined up.'

Robert Holton shook his head. 'I haven't any girl anywhere.'

'Isn't that like life. All the handsome men don't have girls and they wonder why so many of us are old maids.'

'You're not an old maid yet, Marjorie. By the way, what's your last name? As long as I've known you I've never known your last name.'

'Ventusa.' She spelled it for him.

'Italian name.'

'My father was Italian, my mother was Irish.'

'That's a good combination. I knew a lot of pretty girls when I was in Italy.'

'Were you there in the war?'

'I was there over a year.'

'I always wanted to travel. I guess I'd rather travel than do anything. My father, he used to tell me stories about Italy. He came from Sicily. Were you ever in Sicily?'

'Yes, I was in Sicily.'

'It's beautiful, isn't it?'

'Beautiful.'

'Must be real messed up now.'

'Not too bad. The scenery's still there.'

'I'm going to go there someday,' said Marjorie Ventusa, knowing that she never would.

'You'll like it.'

Mrs Merrin was looking at her and she pretended to be busy at his table.

'Let me get you some more coffee,' she said. She picked up the plates from his table and put them on her tray. Her arm touched his hand. He pulled away unconsciously, and she walked back to the kitchen.

She got a cup of coffee for him. Two other orders were ready for her. She put them on her tray and returned to the dining-room.

She noticed a girl was walking over to Robert Holton's table. She had seen the girl often before. She worked in Robert Holton's office. Occasionally they would have lunch together. She was a pretty girl. Her hair was dark and her skin white. Her lips were full and painted a deep red. She had a slim figure and slim legs and her eyes were blue, a deep vivid blue that Marjorie Ventusa envied. The girl spoke to Robert Holton. He stood up. Then they both sat down.

Marjorie Ventusa took care of two tables and then she went to Robert Holton's table and placed his cup of coffee before him.

'Good morning,' she said to the pretty girl.

'Good morning,' said the pretty girl absently. 'I'll have some grapefruit juice. That's all I want. I'm reducing,' she said to Robert Holton and she patted her slim waist.

'What on earth are you reducing for?'

'You think I look all right this way?' she asked, pretending surprise.

Marjorie Ventusa hurried to the kitchen. She hated this pretty girl. All day long Robert Holton was with her. Perhaps even at night they were together. She pushed her blonde hair back out of her face. If only she had been pretty and young. Of course, she had been young but she had never been pretty. She was far from old now. They said that if one wanted something badly enough one would get it. That was foolish; Marjorie Ventusa had never got anything she wanted, except a yellow satin dress. When she was a child she had wanted a yellow satin dress and her father had bought her one. The dress was in a box in her closet now; she had not looked at it in fifteen years. She picked up a glass of grapefruit juice and put it on her tray.

The pretty girl was laughing when she came back to their table and Robert Holton was watching her. She wore a grey suit buttoned tightly across her small breasts.

'Here's your grapefruit juice.'

'Thank you very much,' said the girl, paying no attention to Marjorie Ventusa, saying the words mechanically.

The waitress began to clean the table next to Robert Holton's. She rubbed the grey damp cloth over the shiny black table-top and she listened to Robert Holton and the pretty girl as they talked.

'But Caroline' (her name was Caroline then), 'I didn't know you were expecting me last night.'

'Well, we weren't really. I just thought you might come on over, that's all. We had quite a gang. Jimmy Hammond, he was at Yale about the same time you were.'

'I went to Harvard.'

'That's right, you did. Well, you would've liked Jimmy Hammond. He was in the army, too. And there were a whole lot of people around. I just thought you'd have liked to come.'

'I certainly would've but I didn't remember your inviting me.'

'That's all right,' said Caroline, drinking her grapefruit juice and making a face as she did. 'God, but this stuff is sour.'

Marjorie Ventusa, having cleaned the shiny black table-top cleaner than it had ever been before, turned to another table. She was still close enough to hear what they said.

'What did you do last night, Bobby?' She called him Bobby. Marjorie Ventusa wondered if she would ever be able to call him that.

'Not a thing. I went home to bed early.'

'Next time I'll send you an engraved invitation when I want you to come to the house.'

'You do that. What time's it getting to be?'

Caroline looked at the clock. 'It's not much after eight-thirty. Let's take our time.'

'We don't want to be too late.'

'You haven't been around long. Nobody gets there on time. What're you bucking for, Mr Holton?'

He grinned at her. Robert Holton had dark blue eyes. Marjorie Ventusa had never noticed them before. They were beautiful eyes, she thought suddenly.

One of the waitresses came over to her and said, 'Boy, you sure must like that guy in the corner.'

'What do you mean? What you talking about?'

'Nothing at all. You needn't get so excited. I was just noticing you talking to him all the time. I couldn't help noticing, Marjorie. You was there so long talking to him.'

'He comes in here a lot and we talk, that's all. I hope *you* don't mind.

'I don't mind at all, Marjorie. I was just kidding you.'

Marjorie Ventusa picked up a cup of coffee an went back to the dining-room. The waitress had irritated her. She didn't want anyone to think that she would fall for a man at least ten years younger than she was. Well, perhaps not ten

19

years. Robert Holton could be thirty. The difference between thirty and thirty-seven was not so great.

She walked over to Robert Holton's table. They were talking.

'I don't see what you have against Dick. He's an awful nice fellow.'

'I don't have anything against him. He just doesn't like me. He thinks I'm trying to get his job.'

'Well, are you?'

Robert Holton smiled. 'I don't want anything; didn't you know that?'

'Well, aren't you the saint. You mean you wouldn't like to take his job? Not even if it was offered to you?'

'I suppose if it were easier to take a job than refuse it I'd take the job. I'm easy to please.'

Caroline sighed. 'You're easy to please. I guess that's what war does to you.'

'I was always like that. I was like that at college.'

'Just lazy?'

'Just lazy.'

'Good Lord, it's almost nine! We have to get out of here.'

Robert Holton waved to Marjorie Ventusa. She came over to their table slowly. She didn't want him to leave any sooner than he had to.

'Got my check, Marjorie?'

'I'll get it for you.' She went to the cashier and had his check totalled for him. Then she brought it back and he paid her, leaving a ten-cent tip under his water glass.

Caroline stood up and put her grey coat about her shoulders. Robert Holton picked up his trench coat and slung it over his arm.

'I'll see you at lunch Marjorie,' he said.

'See you,' said Marjorie Ventusa and she watched them as they went out the door into the bright autumn morning.

'Say, Marjorie,' said one of her regular customers, 'how about some more coffee.'

'O.K., O.K.,' she said.

'When are you going to get those tables cleaned?' said Mrs Merrin who was back in Marjorie Ventusa's corner. 'I wish you'd try to get them done right after the customers leave. I wish you'd make some effort, Marjorie.'

'I'm sorry,' said Marjorie Ventusa.

She began to clear Robert Holton's table.

'What about my coffee?' asked the customer. 'When am I going to get it?'

'Right away.' Marjorie Ventusa finished cleaning Robert Holton's table. Almost sadly she pocketed the ten-cent tip which he had left under the water glass.

THREE

The elevator door opened and Caroline Lawson and Robert Holton stepped out of it and into the New York office of Heywood and Golden, members of the New York Stock Exchange and other organizations equally sound.

The entrance hall was modern and dignified. The walls were clean and white and there was a thick carpet on the floor. Two heavy leather couches furnished the entrance. A dark genteel girl sat behind a reception desk.

'Good morning, Caroline,' she said in a nasal voice. 'Good morning, Bob.'

'Hello, Ruth,' said Robert Holton, and Caroline Lawson smiled at her.

'Anything new?' asked Robert Holton.

'Not a thing, Bob, not a thing. Everything's just as dull as ever. Of course, it's still early.'

'Sure,' said Caroline, amused at the thought of anything interesting happening to them, 'the day's just started.'

'Is the boss in yet?' asked Robert Holton. He was terribly afraid of getting in bad, thought Caroline, looking at him. He was rather cowardly but nice. Perhaps having been in the war had changed him. Perhaps he would improve.

Ruth shook her head. 'No, he's not in yet. He hasn't come in yet. He's always late, Mr Murphy is.' Mr Murphy was the head of Statistical Section where Robert Holton worked. Caroline was Mr Murphy's secretary.

'Well, I'm glad,' said Robert Holton.

'You certainly *are* eager,' said Ruth, looking up at him, her head slightly to one side : the way that movie actresses looked.

Robert Holton laughed. 'I guess I am.'

'And after all you've been through, too! Why, if I'd seen what you've seen I wouldn't worry what nob . . . anybody thought.'

'That's what I used to say,' said Robert Holton.

'Come on, Bob,' said Caroline. 'Let's get back to the salt mine.'

Ruth nodded to them and they walked into a long room. On one side of the room were the doors of offices; the other side was covered with tremendous pictures of factories and ships and railroads. The pictures were Mr Golden's idea. He wanted to explain to customers the real meaning of the stocks they were buying. Mr Golden always wanted people to feel that the stock market was a creative, a productive thing.

Women of all ages sat typing at small desks in the long room. The light was indirect and modern and very even. One could see that Heywood and Golden was a well-organized house.

People murmured good mornings to Caroline and Robert Holton as they walked together between the desks. At the end of the room there was a glass door behind which were a large blackboard, tickertape machines, and men recording the prices of the various stocks.

'Look busy, don't they?' commented Caroline.

'They certainly do. I wouldn't have that job for anything.'

'I think it'd be sort of exciting.'

'Too much running around for me. I like to sit still.'

'It takes,' said Caroline, 'all kinds to make up a world.'

'Isn't that lucky?' said Robert Holton and Caroline didn't know whether he was laughing at her or not. Sometimes he bothered her. She liked him. Almost everybody did because he was nice-looking and quiet. He was weak, though, she thought. She didn't like a man to be weak. She wanted some-one that she could lean on. Caroline Lawton was one of those pretty girls who could never bear weak men and yet, by nature, hated those who were stronger.

They stood and watched the tickertape machines through the glass door. A tall white-faced boy was slowly marking figures on the blackboard. He stood on a small stepladder and as he wrote the figures his left foot tapped regularly and rhythmically on the top step of the ladder. Caroline wondered what tune he was making.

'You like to dance, don't you?' she asked suddenly.

'What? Dance? Sure, I like to dance. Why?'

'Oh, I don't know. I was just thinking, that's all. I like to dance a whole lot. When I was at college we used to have wonderful dances.'

Robert Holton laughed. 'That wasn't so long ago, when you were at college. Don't you go out any more?'

'Of course I do. You know I do, all the time, and I'm not trying to get you to ask me out either.'

He laughed at her and that was all.

Caroline looked at him and tried to guess what he was thinking. He was probably thinking that she was very pretty and that he would like to ask her to go out with him. She wouldn't go out with him, he knew. Not now, not after she had said these things. Later, perhaps, when they had forgotten the words she had said. Caroline sighed as she thought of her own strength and of his weakness.

'Let's get back to the office,' said Holton.

They walked down a short corridor. At the end of the corridor was the Statistical room. Here a dozen men and women worked at desks. They compiled figures for the executives and the customers and everyone else in the house.

Through a noise of automatic welcomes, Caroline and Robert Holton went into the office. Most of the desks were on the side of the room away from the windows. The windowed end of the room was protected by a railing; behind the railing was Mr Murphy's desk and at a respectful distance from his desk was Caroline Lawson's.

'See you later, Bob,' said Caroline and she opened the door of the railing and went into the windowed section of the room. She let the door swing creakily shut and went to her desk. Glancing sideways, she watched Robert Holton go to his desk at the other end of the office. Then she sat down.

The desk was neat. A new blotter was in the centre. An inkwell, without ink in it, and a penholder, without a pen in it, held the top of the blotter down. A slim imitation silver vase sat on one corner of the desk. Occasionally Mr Murphy would put a flower in the vase and she would smile at him when he did that and Mr Murphy would wink at her.

One of the two phones on her desk rang. She picked up the receiver. 'Hello?' Someone asked for Mr Murphy. 'He isn't in right now; shall I have him call you? You'll call back later? Thank you.' She cleared her throat, cleared her professional telephone voice away.

She moved the blotter to one end of the desk. Then she lifted the front of her desk and a typewriter appeared. She ran her fingers over the keys, professionally, like a pianist before he begins to play.

She opened the left-hand top drawer of the desk. This was her personal drawer. Here were several compacts in various stages of use. A slightly crushed box of pale green Kleenex, a carton of cigarettes, and a box of fairly expensive candy. The lid of the candy box was off and Caroline Lawson decided that, since her breakfast had been small, a little candy wouldn't hurt her. She picked the largest piece and put it in her mouth.

'Good morning, Caroline. How's the girl?' It was Mr Murphy.

Caroline swallowed quickly. 'Fine, fine, Mr Murphy. How're you today?'

'Me? I'm just fine today. Certainly is a wonderful day today. Makes you feel like going out in the country somewhere. Out to Long Island or some place like that. Go someplace to get away from the city.' Mr Murphy sighed. He had spent all his life in the city and he wanted to go live in the country. He would not like the country, of course, but then he would never leave the city and it made no difference.

'Look what I brought you,' said Mr Murphy. He pulled a slightly rumpled white carnation from his buttonhole. 'We had a big blowout at the Astor last night. It was quite a show we had.'

'Thank you,' said Caroline, smiling at him. She smelled the white flower; a strong odour of cigar smoke spoiled the scent. 'Thank you,' she said again and she put the white flower in the tall vase.

'Any calls? Anything new?'

'You had one call. No message, though. The man said he'd call back later.'

'Good.' Mr Murphy sat down at his desk.

There was a pile of letters on his desk. Very precisely he cut the letters open one by one. Caroline watched him with a mixture of admiration and dislike.

Oliver L. Murphy was a tall man. He was heavy but not in the usual manner. His arms and legs and neck were long and thin and his hips were narrow; his stomach and chest, however, were massive. He held himself erect. His face was red as all Irishmen's faces are supposed to be. His eyes and hair were dark and he had a thick curved nose. Mr Murphy's clothes fitted him well. They were usually of a sombre colour and always correct. His cuffs were beautifully starched.

For five years Caroline Lawson had been his secretary. Her first job had been as his secretary; her last job, too, she thought to herself : she would be married soon and that would be the end of typing and putting cigar-scented flowers in fake silver vases. Caroline Lawson was not sure whom she would marry but she would certainly get married to someone soon.

Mr Murphy finished reading his letters.

'Anything important?' asked Caroline.

Mr Murphy shook his head. 'Not much of anything. We got one letter here I ought to answer.'

'I'll get my pad.' Caroline picked up a lightly ruled pad of paper from her desk. Then she went over and sat down in a chair beside Mr Murphy's desk. She sat close to the window so that the morning sunlight would warm her. As she sat down bits of dust vibrated up into the sunlight from her chair seat. The motes of dust danced and glittered and then slowly sank along the beams of light to the floor.

'I'm ready,' said Caroline Lawson.

Mr Murphy cleared his throat and looked helplessly about him. It was his usual beginning. Then he picked up the letter he was to answer. He waited a moment for the words to come to him.

'Dear,' he began. She made the figure for the word. He

paused, studying the ceiling. He began again, 'Dear Mr Lachum, In reply to your letter of the 16th, etc., etc. . . .' He stopped and closed his eyes; this seemed to help. 'I cannot, I fear, agree with you in your analysis of certain trends now at work . . . no, now abroad in the financial world.' His voice became firm and concise. 'Although I have the greatest personal esteem for the opinions of yourself and associates, uh, in re to the stock market, I must, in this instance, disagree with you, for I am of the opinion that this is a rising market and will continue to be so. All statistics at hand . . . no, available, point to just that. Hoping to hear from you again, and so on.' Mr Murphy stopped and opened his eyes. He looked pleased and exhilarated.

'That's a very nice letter, Mr Murphy. Knowing Mr Lachum, I think you were certainly nice to him.'

'Well, it never does to offend people, Caroline. That's a rule with me. That's something I've always followed. I wouldn't be here today if I hadn't been that way.' He paused and they both thought of a world where there was no Mr Murphy because he had offended people.

'All right, let's hear that letter back.'

Caroline read the letter. Mr Murphy listened, pleased.

'That's fine,' he said when she had finished. 'Type it up please.'

Caroline went back to her desk. The sunlight and the glittering dust were almost out of the room now. Soon they would turn on the fluorescent lights over their desks. Caroline sometimes wished that the morning would last all day.

Caroline put a piece of paper in her typewriter. She started to type; then she remembered that all letters must be done in triplicate. She pulled the sheet of paper out of the machine. Wearily, enjoying her weariness, she arranged more paper in the typewriter.

Her fingers moved swiftly over the keys. She made rhythms as she typed, as the keys clattered on the white paper.

In a few minutes she was finished.

'Very nice,' said Mr Murphy, looking over her shoulder. 'Very nice, indeed. I'll sign that now.'

'O.K.' Caroline took the papers out of the typewriter. She

removed the carbons. Mr Murphy signed the letter carefully. During the last five years Caroline had watched Mr Murphy's signature change. It was becoming more original; the upstrokes were stronger and the 'M' was becoming regal.

She blotted his signature. 'What'll I do next?' she asked.

'I expect you'd better get on with those reports for Mr Golden. He was asking for them yesterday.'

'What *does* he think we are? We were only told to do those reports last week. That takes a lot of time. I don't see what he's always in such a rush for.'

'Well, you know how some people are,' said Mr Murphy, meaning much more than he said.

Caroline nodded wisely. Mr Murphy was often opposed to Mr Golden's business ideas. Mr Heywood, who had inherited a lot of money and never bothered much with business, was Mr Murphy's friend. Mr Golden was a promoter who had become a partner several years before. The conservative element of the house stood firmly against him but his hold over Mr Heywood was equally firm.

'I'll get to work on it right away,' said Caroline.

'Good, I think I'll go up to the front office. If there're any calls tell them I'll call back.'

'Yes, Mr Murphy.'

Smoothly Mr Murphy moved across the room. All of his movements were smooth and swift. He opened the swinging gate that separated him from his staff. They didn't look up from their work as he walked between the desks towards the hall.

Caroline took more paper out of her desk and put it in her typewriter. She opened a black notebook. Slowly she began to copy. After a minute or so she stopped. She wasn't concentrating and she didn't know what was wrong.

Caroline Lawson leaned back in her swivel chair and her arms dropped limply at her sides. The sunlight was gone out of the room and she could no longer see the dust in the light.

Far away she could hear the sounds of automobile horns blowing, of newsboy shouts in the street; and, from time to time, their building would rumble as a train passed under-ground.

Closer to her were the sounds of the office. The clattering of typewriters, the constant low buzz of voices; these were the sounds of her days. Caroline was dissatisfied.

Across the room she could see Robert Holton writing something in a black book. She pitied him because he seemed to really like what he was doing. But then it was better than being a soldier : probably anything was better than that. But then Robert Holton wasn't a woman. That made a lot of difference, thought Caroline. He couldn't be depressed by things the way she was. Men were never sensitive about such things. She had a *malaise*. Having thought of this word, she was pleased with it. The word described her sudden fits of depression.

Robert Holton closed the book on his desk. He looked about him uncertainly. Then he stood up and walked to-wards her. He was presentable, she thought. Certainly better looking than anyone else in Heywood and Golden, but he was not what she wanted at all. Also, there was some doubt in her mind that Robert Holton was interested in her.

'How's it going, Caroline?'

'I'm slowed up.' She sighed loudly and wilted in her chair.

'That's too bad,' he said. She didn't answer. She was quiet for a moment. He watched her and she enjoyed his watching her. Finally he said, 'Murphy's in a good mood today.'

Caroline nodded. 'He's really happy today. He wants to go out in the country. He always wants to do that when he's feeling good.'

'He's some character,' said Robert Holton. He sat down on the railing.

'It would be nice,' said Caroline thoughtfully, 'to go out in the country; have a picnic maybe.'

'Sure, that would be nice, but you couldn't do that.'

'No, I guess *you* couldn't.' Caroline was contemptuous but because she was a very pretty and popular girl she didn't show it. She was sensitive herself and that was what she wanted in life : a man who was as sensitive as she, someone who would respond to her moods. She looked at Robert

29

Holton. He was sitting uneasily on the railing. No, he could never understand her great sadness. Perhaps no one would ever understand her. Caroline was sad, for it is a sad thing to be both pretty and sensitive.

'You're going out tonight, aren't you?'

Robert Holton nodded. 'I'm going to a cocktail party; I'm going to Mrs Raymond Stevanson's.'

'Oh, is that so? You're really going around in high circles. I guess I shouldn't be associating with high society like you.' She had meant to speak lightly and humorously but somehow the words had come out all wrong and there was a bitterness in her voice that embarrassed her.

Robert Holton looked surprised; he smiled finally. 'Well, it never hurts to know these people. She was a friend of my mother's,' he explained, trying to explain these things, to make himself appear like her; she hated him for his kindness.

'Those people are O.K., I guess,' said Caroline. She started to say something about her own family, some improbable but soothing lie, something to prove to herself that she was the same as Mrs Stevanson whose picture was so often in the papers. But she said nothing. She played with the ribbon of her typewriter.

'I hate staying in one place,' said Caroline, after a moment of silence.

'It's no fun travelling,' said Robert Holton. 'Moving around all the time; that's what I didn't like in the army. No, travelling's pretty lousy.'

'That kind is, but I mean to go . . . well, you know . . . where you want to go, that's what I mean. I don't like sitting around here day after day. I want to go some place.'

He shrugged. 'A lot of people do, I guess. Marjorie, you know, the waitress, she wants to go to Sicily.'

'Well, that's different. I mean she's not . . . well, you know what I mean, she's probably happy doing what she's doing.'

'I don't see why,' said Robert Holton. They thought of Marjorie Ventusa for a moment then they didn't think of her again.

Robert Holton shifted his position on the railing. Caroline

looked about the familiar room. The older women were typing and using their adding machines; the younger women were watching Robert Holton; and the younger men (there were three of them) looked up occasionally to see what Caroline was doing. She posed a little for them. She didn't pose haughtily, though. Caroline was too clever for that. She just looked girlish and rather innocent. None of them could understand her sadness and her longing. It pleased her to think how well she hid herself. Not even Robert Holton, talking to her now, could realize these things.

'No,' said Robert Holton, 'no, I want to stay in one place.'

'You don't want to be doing the same thing all the time, do you?'

'I don't know, I'd like to make more money.'

'I think you're crazy,' she said. She watched her fingers as they tapped lightly on the keys of the typewriter. Her hands weren't quite what she wanted them to be. She thought of them as long and slender and faintly exotic; actually her hands were short and square and not very clean. The red enamel was beginning to chip off her thumbnails.

'Why'm I crazy? Because I want to make more money?'

'Not because of that, of course. Just because.'

'Oh.'

Robert Holton shifted his position on the railing. Caroline suddenly didn't want him to go. Then Richard Kuppelton got up from his desk near the door and came over to them.

'Why, hello, Dick,' said Caroline.

'Good morning, good morning,' said Dick heartily. He was a very hearty person and Caroline liked him. He was so different from Robert Holton. Dick always seemed the same; he acted the same, anyway. Caroline could almost always tell what he was going to say that was a lot better than being around a person who never said the right things. Dick wasn't sensitive, however. He and Robert Holton were the same that way but then Caroline couldn't have everything.

'How's every little thing?' asked Dick Kuppelton.

'Fine,' said Robert Holton. Caroline only smiled; she smiled with her eyes as well as her mouth. It was important to smile that way.

31

'Been pretty slow today,' said Dick. 'Not much business. I think the market's falling off.' Someone had told him that, thought Caroline, delighted with her perception.

'It may be,' said Robert Holton without much interest.

'We should have a big rush soon. I'm doing a report now. Well, not really a report; I've been getting some statistics on aircraft stock ready for the front office. It's been some job.' He shook his head to show the largeness of the job.

'I've got a report like that to do, too,' said Caroline.

'Something for Golden?'

'Yes.'

Dick nodded knowingly. 'Some report, I bet.'

'It's certainly long,' said Caroline, pointing to the notebook on her desk.

Robert Holton got off the railing and stretched. 'I better get to work,' he said. 'Murphy might be back soon.' He went back to his desk.

'He's real eager,' said Dick unpleasantly.

'What? Well, I don't know about that. He's sort of funny. He doesn't want to get anywhere but he doesn't want to get in bad. I don't know; he's awful funny.'

'I've seen those guys before,' said Dick. 'I know that type. They come in a place and get in good with the top people. Then they get your job. That's just what he's up to.'

Caroline smiled and said nothing. She was pretty and popular and she couldn't always, therefore, say what she thought. She knew, though, that Dick Kuppelton, who had been with Heywood and Golden for six years, disliked Holton. Mr Murphy had never liked Kuppelton and at the end of the year changes were always made and Robert Holton might take Dick's place. Things were very complicated, thought Caroline.

'I don't think he's that smart,' said Caroline.

'I think you're wrong.' Dick started to straddle the railing, then he changed his mind and leaned against it. He was a large man. He was thirty and pink and blond. He wore large rimless glasses which made his face look clean and blank. He enjoyed what he was doing, thought Caroline. Everyone enjoyed working except herself.

'I've got to do some typing,' said Caroline. She wanted him to go away.

'Certainly; I suppose I'd better be getting back.' He stood up straight and stretched. 'Well, back to work,' he said.

'See you,' said Caroline. Dick was so dependable : you always knew what to expect.

Caroline coughed. Her cough had a consumptive sound to it which rather appealed to her. When she was a young girl she had seen a play about a beautiful woman with white flowers and a cough. The beautiful woman had been so interesting that Caroline had never forgotten her although she had forgotten the play. Caroline coughed again, quietly, dramatically.

'How's that report coming?' Oliver L. Murphy had returned from the front office.

'Pretty well, Mr Murphy.'

'Had quite a session with Mr Golden.'

'I'll bet,' said Caroline with sympathy. 'I'll bet he was something.'

'Well, I handled him O.K. today. He's not so hard to get along with. Of course, he's got some queer ideas. Those people often have.'

'Isn't that the truth.' Caroline arranged the paper in her typewriter. Mr Murphy leaned over and smelled the carnation in the imitation silver vase.

'Smells nice, don't it?'

'It certainly does, Mr Murphy.' She smiled. Mr Murphy went back to his desk and Caroline typed. Several times as she worked she coughed, quietly, almost to herself.

FOUR

Richard Kuppelton left Caroline reluctantly. He liked her because she was pretty and much more sensible than the other pretty girls he had known.

He stopped at his desk. It was a dull olive colour. His different books of statistics were piled neatly on one corner; notebooks and papers were scattered over the top and it looked as if he were busy.

Kuppelton decided not to work, not just now. From the top drawer of his desk he took a magazine. It had a vivid cover of a large-breasted young woman being carried into a machine by an octopus. He enjoyed this magazine's stories very much.

He slipped the magazine under his arm, the cover towards his side; and then, busily, he left the room for the lavatory.

There was something cozy about a lavatory, he thought as he opened the door marked 'Men'. No one was inside and he would be able to sing. The room was large, white and very clean. The urinals, four of them, stood polished and shining, like soldiers on guard. A thin waterfall constantly descended down their white enamel surfaces; the smell of disinfectant was in the air, but not too strongly.

Richard Kuppelton glanced at himself quickly in one of the four mirrors which shone over the four wash basins. Then he walked to one of the four black-doored stalls. He chose the one nearest the wall. There was strategy in his choice as well as habit, for the light was over this stall.

With the feeling of having come home after a long journey, Richard Kuppelton opened the black door and stepped inside. Then he closed the door and locked it. He was completely alone now; no one could disturb him and he was safe.

Deliberately he hung up his coat and then, after some preparation, he descended with a sigh upon the cool smooth seat. He relaxed happily.

On the subway he had started a story called 'The Mad Moon Maidens'; unfortunately, it had been a little dull and he had decided not to finish it. He thumbed through the rough pages of his magazine. Grotesque black and white drawings decorated the pages. There were monsters and ghouls, beautiful women (usually screaming) and lean young men with pongee hats. The title 'Satan Underworld' appealed to him and he started to read.

After only a few minutes, however, he found himself studying the tile floor. Black and white tile in neat one-two-three pattern across the floor; he liked things that were black or white. The pattern was familiar to him and gave him a further feeling of being home.

Great ideas came to Richard Kuppelton enthroned. Here in this retreat the entire world assumed a pattern of great simplicity. All problems could be rendered answerable and in this world he was sovereign. The lavatory was his study. He thought of Robert Holton : the person who currently threatened his career.

Robert Holton was deceitful; he knew that. On the surface he appeared simple and a little shy but Kuppelton knew differently. Little things that the others had not noticed he noticed. For instance, Holton was always trying to get friendly with Mr Murphy. He always called him 'sir'; treated him as if he were a colonel or something in the army. That was another thing : the army. Holton had been a soldier and Kuppelton had not. Most of the others in the office had not been in the war either. Both Mr Heywood and Mr Golden had declared that they would do all that they could for the veteran. So far this hadn't been very much, but still it was their intention. Richard Kuppelton wished suddenly that he could stay forever in this shiny black stall with the tile floor.

There was a noise in the lavatory. Someone had come in. Footsteps clattered on the floor. The door to the stall next to his opened and someone sat down.

He wondered who it was. The person wore plain brown shoes : he could see them through the foot-high space beneath the stall partition. This person also wore brown trousers. Richard Kuppelton thought for a moment, strained to remember who it could be. Then he remembered.

'Hello, Bob,' said Richard Kuppelton.

'What? That you, Dick?'

'The same.'

'You catching up on your reading?'

Richard Kuppelton closed his magazine guiltily. 'No, no. Just nature.'

'It's a good place to think.'

'Well, I suppose it is.'

'What's wrong with Caroline today?' asked Robert Holton.

'I haven't the slightest idea. I didn't notice anything wrong with her did you?'

'Yes, I thought she was sort of irritable.'

'I didn't notice it.' Richard Kuppelton sighed. He was beginning to get uncomfortable, sitting on the hard seat. He was, also, a little surprised that Holton was as aware of Caroline as this. 'Caroline's a lot of fun,' he said.

'Yes.'

'She's a lot of fun to go out on a party with. She can be real funny.'

'I suppose so.'

'You ever go out with her?'

'Not really.'

'What do you mean?'

'I never went to a party with her. We had dinner once.'

'She didn't want to go dancing?'

'No.'

'That's funny.' Richard Kuppelton tried to remember whether he had ever taken Caroline out and they had not danced. No, they had always gone to a dance. He wondered whether she liked Robert Holton better than him. This was a new thought and even more unpleasant than the suspicion that Robert Holton was trying to get his job. 'She just likes to talk?'

36

'Yes, I guess everybody does.'

'That's right, I guess.' Richard Kuppelton studied Holton's plain tan shoes gloomily. One of the things he could not understand was why Robert Holton had come to work in this office. It was rumoured that he was a friend of Mr Heywood's but no one had ever been able to prove that. He had gone to Harvard before the war and to Richard Kuppelton that was the most important thing about him. It was also suspicious; he could not understand why a person with that education would do this job in Heywood and Golden unless – and Richard Kuppelton became gloomier – unless he were to be promoted over everyone.

'Looks like there'll be a lot of changes after the first,' said Kuppelton.

'They tell me there usually are.'

'I suppose you want to end up in the other office, being one of the contact people.'

'I don't care much. Whatever they want to do. I'd like to move up, of course.'

'We all would.'

Robert Holton mumbled something and stood up. Kuppelton watched the tan shoes as they moved about the stall. There was a swirling of water and Robert Holton left the lavatory, whistling.

Richard Kuppelton studied the tile again. It seemed, somehow, less comforting, less private since Holton had been here. He tried to read again but 'Satanic Underworld' had lost its attraction. The seat was becoming harder every minute and he would have to leave soon.

Then he remembered that the acoustics were unusually good in this lavatory. In a low voice he sang an Irish ballad which he had learned in school. His voice came to him pure and vibrant and like no other voice that had ever sung. He finished with a low note, although, strictly speaking, the ballad called for a high note. He sang a popular song next. It was not as great a success as the first because he only knew the chorus. The words that he made up, however, were quite good enough.

At last, his songs finished, Richard Kuppelton stood up.

He ached slightly from the strain of sitting on the narrow seat. Deliberately he arranged his trousers, deploring slightly the heaviness of his waist as he did.

The sound of swirling water was in his ears as he crossed the lavatory to the wash basin. Deliberately – he was a deliberate person – he washed his hands. He dried his hands on a paper towel and then, like a king abdicating, he moved slowly but deliberately to the door. With a sigh Richard Kuppelton left the lavatory.

The office had not changed. Mr Murphy was sitting behind his railing, smoking a cigar and reading a letter. Caroline was typing. Robert Holton was copying a row of figures into his note book. The other men and women in the office were working busily.

Richard Kuppelton sat down at his desk. He enjoyed the sensation of being a part of this great house. Neatly he arranged his books of tables and statistics across the top of his desk. The various books were open at aircraft stock. His statistics would form the basis of a report which would be used in an overall survey of aircraft stock to be used by the front office. His responsibilities were heavy.

He took his fountain pen out of his pocket. It was leaking a little and he had to handle it carefully. Slowly, with pleasure, he copied the figures from the books. He wrote the numbers carefully, making them round and legible. When he had finished copying all his numbers they would be typed up by one of the stenographers in the office.

A tall white-faced boy in a blue suit came into the room. He went to Richard Kuppelton's desk and put some papers on it.

'Good morning, Jim,' said Kuppelton heartily. 'How's the boy?'

'Fine. I think Golden's coming this way.'

'Really? Wonder what he wants.'

'Hard to say. He always wants something.'

'That's his privilege,' said Kuppelton righteously.

'I suppose so,' said Jim.

The white-faced boy went on to the next desk, handing out letters and inter-office memoranda.

Richard Kuppelton put his fountain pen down carefully. There were several letters for him. He opened one of them and started to read.

He had read only a few lines when Mr Golden came into the office. Even without looking up from his letter Richard Kuppelton could have told that someone from the front office had arrived. The typewriters clattered more loudly. The usual low buzz of voices died away, and he could hear Mr Murphy's swivel chair being pushed back from his desk as he stood up to welcome the visitor from the front office. Kuppelton put his letter under the blotter and then he looked up casually.

Benjamin Franklin Golden stood behind Mr Murphy's railing. He stood very erect, his eyes moving from desk to desk as he studied the office. He was a short man and plump. His eyes were small and black and shiny. Mr Golden had iron-grey hair which he allowed to grow a little longer than necessary. He was proud to have kept his hair. He had a small nose and a rather foolish little mouth and he looked more like a South American or Italian or something like that, thought Kuppelton.

He pretended to write figures in his notebook, while he listened carefully to what Mr Golden was saying to Mr Murphy.

'Everything all right here, Murphy?' Mr Golden had a high thin voice.

'Yes, sir, we're getting your reports out. I'll have the special one for you this afternoon.'

'That's good. I really need that report. That's an important one. Some of our big steel clients are interested in it. I know you've done a good job on it.' There was almost a threat in his voice. It was well known that the two did not like each other.

'Well, I've got our best girl, I've got Caroline here typing it.' He waved at Caroline who looked up and smiled at Mr Golden who smiled back at her. Richard Kuppelton wondered what Mrs Golden was like.

'I'm sure she'll do a good job. How's that aircraft stock report coming?'

39

'Kuppelton's doing it.' Mr Murphy pointed to him.

Mr Golden nodded. 'I'll be interested to see it.' Richard Kuppelton copied figures quickly.

'Should be a good survey,' said Mr Murphy. 'Is there going to be a board meeting this morning? You said they hadn't decided earlier.'

'Oh, yes, I almost forgot; there'll be a meeting at eleven-thirty.' Mr Golden had an irritatingly brusque manner.

'Fine,' said Mr Murphy and he made a note of it on the pad on his desk.

Mr Golden didn't seem to want to go. He looked around the room again. He looked at Robert Holton and said something to Mr Murphy which Kuppelton couldn't hear. Mr Murphy smiled and nodded.

Mr Golden finally opened the door of the railing. 'See you at the meeting, Murphy.'

'Yes, sir.'

Mr Golden hurried out of the office. There was an immediate change in the sounds of the room after he had left. The hum of voices began again. Richard Kuppelton put down his fountain pen.

Caroline and Mr Murphy were talking together and laughing. Robert Holton was still working quietly at his desk. The women of the office talked about Mr Golden in low voices.

Richard Kuppelton wondered what Mr Golden had said to Mr Murphy about Robert Holton. He looked at Robert Holton with dislike.

'O.K.,' said Kuppelton, 'Mr Golden's gone, you can stop working.'

Robert Holton put down his notebook and smiled. 'It doesn't hurt,' he said. 'It doesn't hurt to look busy.'

'Oh, no, I wasn't meaning to criticize.'

'I didn't think you were. Did you hear what they were talking about?'

This was malicious, Richard Kuppelton knew it; it would have been very hard for Holton not to have heard. 'Oh, they were just talking about reports.'

'That's what I guessed.' He started to work again.

'You live uptown, don't you?' remarked Kuppelton.

'Yes. I've got a room in a hotel.'

'That's funny, I thought you lived with your family or something. I thought Caroline said something about it.'

'My father used to live here. He lives in Boston now. He used to work here but he retired when I got out of the army.'

Richard Kuppelton nodded. 'That's right, I remember your telling me that once. Me, I live with all my family in Queens. We all live there. I wish sometimes that I lived alone.'

'It's not much fun, living alone,' said Robert Holton.

'Think you'll get married soon?'

'I don't think so.'

'I think *I* might,' said Richard Kuppelton weightily; he had no one in mind, though; except possibly Caroline.

'I guess it's a good idea if you've got the right person,' said Robert Holton.

'That's very true.' They thought of this a moment. Each thought of it seriously and each regarded it distantly. Richard Kuppelton had no real desire to be married. He supposed that Robert Holton felt the same.

'I wonder,' said Kuppelton subtly, 'what the conference is going to be about this afternoon. I wonder if it's about promotions in the departments.'

'I haven't any idea.'

'Since the war, seniority doesn't make much difference.'

'I thought it did.'

Kuppelton shook his head, convinced of Holton's insincerity. For weeks now everyone had discussed the new policy and everyone had watched the veterans in the different offices, especially Holton; it was expected that they would all be promoted : in any event Holton would be.

'No, it doesn't make a bit of difference.'

Robert Holton smiled. He had small white teeth and an agreeable smile which Kuppelton resented. 'That's good news for me. I haven't been here very long you know.'

'Oh, yes, I know,' and Kuppelton laughed loudly to show that he was friendly and that it made no difference to him who was promoted.

He glanced towards the windows. Mr Murphy caught his eye and motioned to him. Quickly Richard Kuppelton got to his feet and walked across the room to the railing. He was careful not to let the gate slam when he came into Mr Murphy's presence.

'Yes, sir?'

'I just wanted to check with you on that aircraft stock report. I just wanted to make sure it was coming along well.'

'I've been working on it right along, Mr Murphy. They'll start typing it up tomorrow.'

Murphy compressed his lips and nodded slowly. 'Mr Golden was asking for it. I wanted to be sure, Dick.'

Kuppelton was suddenly glad that Mr Murphy had called him by his first name. He did this only when he was well pleased or when he wanted something.

'It's been quite a job getting those things together but I finally . . . got them together.'

'I know how it is. How's your family these days?'

'They're pretty well. My mother's been better. Her legs don't bother her so much now.'

'That's good. Arthritis is pretty bad. I had a grandmother who had it once.'

'It's pretty bad,' agreed Richard Kuppelton.

They both paused and wondered what to say next. Kuppelton began to edge towards the gate. Murphy stood up. 'Let me see that thing as soon as you get it done.'

'I certainly will.'

Mr Murphy turned to Caroline who was typing at her desk. 'I'm going to be in conference for a while,' he said. 'Take care of the calls, will you?'

'Yes, Mr Murphy.'

'Big conference?' asked Kuppelton when Murphy had gone.

'I don't know,' said Caroline and she stopped typing. 'They were talking about it. Something to do with policy, I think.'

Caroline got up from her desk and stretched. She had nice slim legs, Kuppelton noticed. He wondered if his mother would like her. It was important to him to have his mother

42

like his future wife – if he ever had one. She had been wonderful about the other girls he had liked but somehow they had never been quite what she thought his wife should be. He was her favourite son and he could not disappoint her, naturally.

'I guess that leaves me out,' he said wearily, hoping she would give him some good news.

'Well, I wouldn't worry too much,' she said, a little coldly he thought, 'you've got a good job now.'

'Well, you're right about that,' he said emphatically.

'Oh, I know I am. Bob's the fair-haired boy these days,' she added.

'I expect he is.'

Caroline walked to the window and looked down at the crowded street. 'There really are a lot of people in this town,' she said in a distant voice.

'There sure are.'

'Do you ever wonder about all those people . . . down there?'

This was the sort of talk that made Richard Kuppelton nervous. He hated it when people started asking him vague questions to which there were no sensible answers. 'No, I can't say that I do.'

She turned around and looked at him then, looked at him rather sadly, he thought. 'I've got work to do,' was all she said.

'See you, Caroline.'

Robert Holton was leaning back in his chair.

'Pretty dull, isn't it?' commented Dick.

'The army was a lot duller.'

'I thought that was one thing that it wasn't . . . dull.'

Robert Holton chuckled. 'This is a lot better.'

'Don't you miss moving around?'

He paused before he replied and Kuppelton wondered what the truth really was; however, Robert Holton only said, 'No, no, I like staying in one place.'

Richard Kuppelton turned back to his books of figures. He wondered helplessly, as he wrote, how anyone could be as deceitful as Robert Holton. It was obvious to him that Holton would get the job he was to have got and he certainly could not get this job without being deceitful. Richard Kuppelton was worried about this. He was also worried because he found himself hating Robert Holton and his mother would never have approved of that.

FIVE

The ulcer was the most important thing.

After the ulcer his wife, and then his job, and finally his children. These were Mr Murphy's interests. At the moment the ulcer was more important to him than all the others together.

Ever since Mr Murphy could remember, he had had pains in his stomach. Not really bad pains : just unpleasant sensations. In recent years this had got worse. A month before, a doctor examined him and said that he had an ulcer. The doctor was very serious and there was talk of further tests. Then Mr Murphy read a picture magazine article on cancer.

He did not suspect cancer : he knew. The doctor, although he had been rather grave, had said nothing about cancer, but Mr Murphy was confident he had it. He had tried to do everything right, to cure himself with bicarbonate of soda and other medicines but the pains not only didn't go away but they got worse when he thought about them.

He pushed his fist into his stomach for a moment and felt the pain under his fingers. He cursed himself for having gone to the party the night before.

As he walked through his office he wished that he were home in bed. It would have been harder, of course, to stay home, because his wife was not very good with an illness. She had a tendency to become hysterical if she had to do anything unusual. No, it was better to be here at the office. To be here even if he was dying. This last thought made him uncomfortable and he put it out of his mind.

He looked at his watch – eleven-fifteen. The meeting would begin soon. Mr Golden insisted that all meetings began on time.

Mr Murphy left his office. As he walked through the rooms he was pleased to have everyone speak to him politely. He was a person of importance here and he had become this all by himself with no help from anyone; practically no help.

The executive offices were larger and better decorated than the other offices. There were several uniform rooms where the vice-presidents (they used to be partners but Mr Golden had changed that) sat at big desks and received clients and dictated letters and did other things. Then there was the anteroom. This was a small room with red leather couches, a receptionist, some modern lamps and two portraits on the walls. These paintings were of Mr Heywood and Mr Golden. Beyond the anteroom was the boardroom.

The receptionist smiled at Mr Murphy. He smiled back at her and sat down in one of the red leather couches. Two minor vice-presidents were also seated and waiting. They greeted him soberly.

'Nice morning,' said the younger of the vice-presidents; he had been a lieutenant commander in the navy.

'Certainly is,' said Mr Murphy.

'I understand we're in for a cold winter,' commented the older of the two vice-presidents; he had been a commander in the navy.

'Nothing like a real old-fashioned Christmas,' said Mr Murphy in a smooth low voice. He was conscious of a difference in their voices. His own voice sounded rough to him while their voices were always smooth and almost British. He had noticed these differences before but there was nothing much he could do about them. In the front office he always felt less important because of this difference, and because of this and other things, too, he was made to feel an outsider.

The vice-presidents then talked in their cultured near-British voices about a certain college football game. Mr Murphy lay back in his red couch and wondered if perhaps he should drink more milk. That was good for ulcers; but nothing was good for cancer. He shuddered.

A few more vice-presidents and section heads came into the anteroom. They talked and laughed together and

Oliver L. Murphy talked and laughed with them.

There was a buzz and everyone stopped talking. The receptionist looked up from her desk. 'They're ready,' she said.

The men walked into the boardroom of Heywood and Golden.

A long room, with indirect lighting, thick carpets, and a long table with armchairs around it : this was the boardroom. On the walls were charts of stocks and trends.

Mr Heywood was sitting at one end of the table and Mr Golden was sitting at the other end of the table. Murphy sat down on the left of Mr Heywood. This was his usual seat.

'Hello, Oliver,' said Mr Heywood cheerily.

'Hello, Mr Heywood.' Murphy was suddenly glad, glad that Mr Heywood had called him by his first name; he did this only when he was well-pleased, or wanted something.

Oliver L. Murphy leaned back in his leather armchair. Mr Heywood sat rather limply on his own chair at the head of the table. He waited for the others to be seated.

Lawrence Heywood was a gentleman. He had a large estate in Maryland and he collected prints; he had had three wives and a number of children and, generally, he had managed to do everything in a large but tasteful manner.

He was a tall man in his late forties. Completely bald, his neat round head shone pinkly under the indirect lights. His face was smooth and neat and looked as if he had never worried in his life. His voice was not near-British like his vice-presidents : it was British. He had gone to school in Massachusetts which explained a lot of it, thought Murphy.

Mr Heywood did everything properly. He had inherited a lot of money. It seemed as if every year a new relative would die and leave more money to him. His three wives had all been beautiful and that was another thing to be said for him – he knew how to choose women. Mr Murphy wondered what it would be like to marry a beautiful woman.

'How's that new man in your office?' asked Mr Heywood suddenly.

'You mean Holton? He's doing very well.'

'I'm glad to hear it. We have a mutual friend,' and Mr Heywood laughed gently at the thought.

'Is that right? He's got a good background, I guess,' said Murphy.

'I expect so. I used to know his mother. She was a very attractive woman twenty years ago. She married . . .' Mr Heywood decided not to reminisce in front of Murphy.

'He's worked in my section, in the office, just fine.'

'That's good. I don't know him myself but I have some plans for him. We're going to the same party tonight.' Mr Heywood laughed gently again. 'Perhaps we'll get to know each other. It's so hard ever getting to know employees in the office,' sighed Mr Heywood. 'I rather wish there weren't so many of them sometimes.'

'I know just how it is.'

'We going to call this meeting together?' It was Mr Golden's high voice from the other end of the table.

'Certainly, Ben,' said Mr Heywood. 'We'll start right now.' He picked up a black ebony gavel and tapped lightly, apologetically with it. The men stopped talking. 'Now, let's see,' began Mr Heywood.

'The Steel account, that's the big thing we're going to talk about,' said Mr Golden.

'That's right.' Mr Heywood sounded bored. 'That's right. Well, gentlemen, it seems that we have a problem.'

Mr Murphy relaxed in his chair. Mr Heywood's voice, gentle and cultured, came to him soothingly. The Steel account was of no interest to Mr Murphy; in fact, these conferences were generally of no interest to him. He was just there to talk about Statistics.

He played with papers in front of him. The voice of Mr Heywood flowed about him. He was lost in a slow current of polite vowels. The pain in his stomach was for the time, gone.

Mr Heywood spoke of the market, of stocks and shares, of the state of the Union. He spoke convincingly because his manner was convincing and, also, because his ideas and facts had been given him by many clever men.

Mr Golden sat at his end of the table and listened. He sat there very straight, his little mouth set in a soft line of pseudo-firmness. His small hands drummed on the table and his eyes

48

glanced about the room. His eyes were always in motion. The fear of a thousand years was in Mr Golden's eyes.

From time to time he interrupted. Mr Heywood would pause and listen; then, when the other had finished, he would continue in his gentle voice to tell the others what clever men had told him about Steel, and the men, whose livings depended upon him, listened respectfully to their ideas.

Mr Murphy observed these things as he sat in his chair. He felt less important in these conferences but he did feel secure. Here in the boardroom he felt himself to be a part of something large and opulent – of American Business. This thought was comforting as well as sobering. There was no security in the world to equal that of belonging. It made no difference to what one belonged just as long as one was a part of something big and secure. And what, Oliver Murphy asked himself, could be bigger or more secure than Business? He saw these things clearly because he had a philosopher's mind and the Celt's ability to envisage life in a clear perspective. He could, he knew, see the trees as well as the forest. That was what made him different from the others. They felt, perhaps, that they belonged, but he *knew*.

Then the ulcer began to bother him.

He no longer was conscious of Mr Heywood's voice. The only thing of importance now was the dull pain in his stomach. He moved uneasily in his chair. He pushed a hand into his stomach. This helped a little. The pain shifted slightly. He followed it with his hand, his fingers pressing gently into the pain.

'We'll want complete figures on the rise and fall of Arizona Zinc during the past five years.'

This was said by Mr Heywood. It registered in Mr Murphy's mind but he didn't respond for a moment.

'You'll have those figures for us next meeting, won't you?' Heywood asked, irritation in his voice.

'Certainly, Mr Heywood,' said Murphy. He sat up straight and Mr Heywood nodded to him and then continued to talk.

Oliver Murphy listened carefully to everything said. He was beginning to sweat from the pain and the fear (more fear than pain, he told himself) but still he strained to hear every word and, slowly, as he listened, magic took place and the pain went away.

At last, when certain decisions had been made, Mr Heywood adjourned the meeting.

Murphy stood up. He felt better now. He wondered if perhaps he might not be mistaken about the cancer.

'Oh, Murphy.'

'Yes, Mr Heywood?'

'That fellow in your office, that Holton, you think he's quite efficient?'

'I do.'

'I wonder,' said Mr Heywood hesitantly, 'I wonder how he might work out as one of our customers' men. Dealing with the public, all that sort of thing.'

'He'd probably do that very well.'

'You could afford to lose him?'

'Oh, yes, I think so.'

'I wish,' said Mr Heywood petulantly, 'that I knew him better. It's terrible having so little contact with the office people.'

'I could send him in to see you.'

'Good Lord, no! I wouldn't know what to say. I'll wait and see him tonight at Mrs Stevanson's.'

'When do you think you'll change him over?'

'Oh, I don't know. If I think he has the suitable, ah, temperament, we might change him this week.'

'I know he'll be really tickled to hear this.'

'I expect so.'

'How is Mrs Heywood?' asked Murphy politely.

'She's fine, thank you,' said Mr Heywood blankly. Trouble, decided Murphy. The third Mrs Heywood seemed to be following the previous Mrs Heywoods.

'Well . . .' said Murphy and he mumbled words to himself as he walked towards the door. Mr Heywood stared vacantly at him as he left.

Mr Murphy felt well when he was in motion. Walking with great dignity from office to office, conscious of the eyes of others upon him, was good for him. Aware of being a symbol of success he forgot his pains and some of his worries.

As he went into the Statistical office he could feel the atmosphere change. The clerks and typists became busy.

Mr Murphy went to his desk. 'Any calls?' he asked.

Caroline shook her head. When she shook, her breasts quivered slightly. Mr Murphy noticed this and his stomach constricted with pain. Emotion was bad for him, according to the doctors. He looked away and tried to think of something else.

'No, there weren't any calls. Some memorandums came in from the other sections but that was all.'

'Any letters?' He thought of his family.

'Yes.' Caroline sounded surprised. 'Right there on your desk. Right where I always put them.'

'Oh, yes.' Mr Murphy sat down at his desk and looked at the pile of neat businesslike envelopes. He had no desire to open them.

Caroline typed rhythmically at her desk.

'Say, Caroline . . .'

She stopped and looked at him.

'Tell Holton to step over here, will you?'

'Sure, Mr Murphy.' She got up and went through the gate and out into the office. He watched her legs as she walked determinedly to the other end of the room. He was almost pleased to feel the pain come flooding into his stomach. That would teach his stomach, he thought viciously.

The gate creaked and Robert Holton stood before him.

'You want to see me, sir?'

'Yes, yes, Holton. Sit down here. Over here on my left.'

Robert Holton sat down and looked expectant. Mr Murphy wondered for a moment why he had asked to see Holton. Then he remembered what Mr Heywood had said.

'How's everything coming, Holton?'

'Just fine, Mr Murphy.'

'Well, that's good. Things *have* been going pretty well here. But I suppose you find things pretty dull after the army?'

'No, no. I like this sort of work. I had enough moving around.'

'I should think so. Well, that's what most of us want, I guess,' said Mr Murphy. 'We want to settle down. A lot of people say they don't like routine but I think everybody does. It's an important thing.'

'Yes, sir. I think it is.'

'There is,' said Mr Murphy, shutting his eyes for a moment to give the illusion of pondering, 'there is security in working for a big house like Heywood and Golden.' He opened his eyes and looked directly at Holton. 'Don't you feel that's true?'

'Yes, I hope so.'

'Yes, it's true.' Mr Murphy sighed and thought about going out to the country for a rest. A place that would have neither telephones nor mosquitoes. Most places had one or the other.

He looked at Robert Holton and wondered what he was thinking. He seemed a likeable young man. He was quiet and reserved and didn't seem too agressive. In fact that was probably a fault that Mr Murphy had not thought of. Holton was not a go-getter. He might lack initiative. That was why he was quiet and reserved. Or, as Mr Murphy finally thought, that might be a reason for his reserve.

'Tell me, Holton,' said Murphy, 'have you had any ideas about, ah, your place here? I mean, what you would like to do. Naturally you wouldn't be interested in staying here, in this department. With your education . . .' He permitted his voice to fade.

'No, I haven't had any ideas; in fact, I haven't thought too much about it. You see this is all pretty different from what it was like where I was in the army. I don't suppose I'm quite used to the idea . . . well, you know . . .'

'I think I do. You would like to work in another department perhaps?'

Robert Holton looked at him. Mr Murphy could not tell what he was thinking for his face was relaxed and calm. 'Well,' said Holton, 'I don't know. I don't want to be out of my depth. I'd like to make more money. I like the idea of buying and selling stocks. I like that idea very much. In fact, that's one of the reasons I came here.'

52

'Of course, there's a lot of work to knowing about stocks and bonds. You realize all the work that's involved.'

'Yes.'

'Perhaps a place will be found for you in that department. It's hard to say, though. With your, ah, background it shouldn't be too hard. That is, if you have the stuff.'

'I hope so.'

'Good.' Mr Murphy watched Caroline typing. 'I understand,' said Mr Murphy finally in a changed voice, 'that you're going out tonight.'

Robert Holton looked surprised. 'What do you mean?'

'Mr Heywood said you and he were going to the same party.'

Holton smiled. 'That's right. I'd forgotten. Mrs Stevanson's giving a cocktail party. I guess that's what he means.'

'It won't hurt to be nice to him there,' said Mr Murphy with a laugh.

'No, I don't suppose so.'

Mr Murphy looked at Holton and wondered what would become of him. If he had more initiative he might be a wealthy man because of his background (the important thing was background), but he would probably not go very far. He might not even go as far as Mr Murphy had and Mr Murphy had been a success without background. Robert Holton didn't look as though he cared to be a success.

'Well, don't let your night life interfere with business,' said Mr Murphy lightly.

'No,' said Holton rising, 'I won't.'

With a nod Mr Murphy dismissed him.

Mr Murphy watched Caroline absently as she typed. Her hair was rather long. It might be a nuisance to help her into a coat, he thought suddenly. That was something he hated to do. Whenever he helped a woman into a coat there was, first, a certain struggle to get her arms into the sleeves. Some women were better than others at this. And then, second, there was the problem of hair. If the woman had long hair it was inevitably caught inside the coat. This meant that her first motion was usually to free her hair and that involved a wild freeing and flinging of the hair which for anyone still

53

posted behind her meant running a risk of becoming entangled. Mr Murphy wondered about these problems as he looked at Caroline's long dark hair.

He had started to work on his letters (the ones in the business envelopes) when Richard Kuppelton appeared.

'Yes?'

'I've got the first part of the report here, the one on aircraft,' said Kuppelton.

'Yes?' Mr Murphy made himself sound cold and official.

'Well, I wondered if you cared to look at them . . . what I've done so far, I mean.'

Mr Murphy looked at him for a moment without speaking. When Mr Murphy had first come to work for Heywood and Golden his then immediate boss had impressed him greatly by just looking at him for several seconds at a time without speaking. Mr Murphy had adopted the mannerism and over the years had improved it until now he could be very frightening. He was that way now.

'You want me to do it for you?' he asked finally.

'No . . . no, sir, I didn't mean that. I just thought you would like to see what I got done.' Kuppelton was uncomfortable and Mr Murphy decided that he had done enough.

'Why, I'd be glad to look at it,' he said.

Kuppelton brightened. 'Thank you. I only wanted you to see the form I was using here. That was all. I'm making my conclusions in a slightly different way from usual and I thought . . .'

'Yes, I'll take a look at it.'

Kuppelton put a pile of papers down on Mr Murphy's desk.

Mr Murphy nodded at him and Kuppelton left quickly. Mr Murphy felt much better after exercising his power. Poor Kuppelton was a good man in an office but he would never go very far because he didn't have assurance. He would be promoted after the first of the year if Holton were moved out. That would make Kuppelton happy, which was a good thing. It wasn't bad, thought Mr Murphy, to have contented people about you in a discontented world. He relaxed in his chair and then the pains started again.

54

This time the ache was about an inch below his belt and slightly towards the left (his appendix was on the right and, besides, his appendix was in good shape). The pain began to move towards the centre. Quickly he pressed his fingers into the pain.

His heart beat rapidly and sweat formed on his face. If the pain didn't go away by the count of ten he would get up and take the special medicine his doctor had given him.

Frightened, Mr Murphy counted and the pain, not subject to this magic, did not go away.

SIX

'It's twelve o'clock,' Caroline said to Mr Murphy. 'I think I'll go out to lunch, if that's O.K.'

'Yes, yes, Caroline.'

She thought he looked rather pale. She was about to ask him how he felt but she stopped herself, remembering how he disliked talking about his health. She had noticed that during the last year he had been taking a lot of medicine. Perhaps he was going to die. Caroline began to compose a little drama to herself. Mr Murphy had just collapsed across his desk and she had been the only one to keep a clear head . . .

'You coming, Caroline?' It was Robert Holton.

'Be right there.' She arranged the papers on her desk, shut the drawers and joined Robert Holton outside the gate of the railing.

'Where'll we eat today?' asked Holton.

'At *the* restaurant, of course. Where did you think we would?'

'Oh, I don't know.' He was smiling now and she wondered if he could have been trying to be funny; she could never be sure.

'Sometimes you don't make sense,' said Caroline.

They were almost through the door when one of the secretaries called to Holton. 'Phone, Bob.'

She waited for him at the door. He went over to his desk and answered the phone. He seemed excited, she noticed, and he talked very quickly. She wished she could hear what he was saying. Finally, he finished and joined her.

'Who was that?'

'An old friend of mine.'

'Man or woman?'

'A guy I used to know. He just got in town. He comes from out West and I haven't seen him for a couple of years.'

'You knew him in the army?'

'Yes.'

They walked through the offices to the elevator and Holton pressed the button.

'What's he doing in town?'

'He's just visiting. I'm going to see him this afternoon. He's coming over here after lunch.'

'That'll be nice. What does he look like?' She asked this gaily, hoping to have some effect on him. She didn't, though.

'I don't know. He looks all right, I guess.'

'You certainly are good at description. Be sure to let me meet him.

'I will.'

The elevator stopped for them and they pushed into the lunch-going crowd. With a rush they descended to the street floor.

Outside the sun shone brightly above the street. The sky was a vivid blue and the air smelt clean in spite of the exhaust fumes and the people of the city. The day was warm.

They walked along the crowded street. Men of affairs with brief cases walked in and out of swinging glass doors. Younger men of affairs, wearing bowler hats and dark coats with darker velvet lapels, marched solemnly in the parade of business. The white-faced clerks squinted at the bright sun. Women secretaries walked together, admiring themselves in the windows. As they walked they talked to each other and to themselves.

'What a nice day,' said Caroline, breathing deeply and coughing as the exhaust fumes tickled her throat.

'Must be nice in the country,' commented Robert Holton.

'Not you too?' Caroline laughed. 'First Murphy and now you want to go out in the country.'

'I don't want to go. I just said it must be pleasant there.' They crossed a street and he looked carefully to left and right and when they finally crossed the street the crowd had gone

57

around them and the light was beginning to change again.

'Why do you take so long?' said Caroline disagreeably.

'Just careful, that's all.'

They walked in silence then. She was very conscious of his being beside her, of her arm being in his. This troubled Caroline, this awareness. She looked at Holton's face as they walked down the crowded street. There was nothing in his face that she would like to have seen. This made her feel better because he was not the right person.

Over the high grey buildings was a narrow section of bright blue sky. It was almost too bright and contrasted strangely with the dingy buildings and the dark streets. Caroline watched the blue sky suspended upon the buildings. No clouds were in the sky but from time to time a bird would circle in it. And, as she watched the sky, a large airliner, like a rigid bird, moved straightly eastward.

Caroline breathed deeply again, careful this time not to get the exhaust fumes too far down in her lungs. She coughed anyway.

Marjorie Ventusa looked through the plate-glass window at the street. She had been watching off and on for half an hour, waiting for Robert Holton to come.

Some days he would come in at twelve and other days at twelve-thirty, and then there had been certain days when he'd not come in at all and those were bad days for Marjorie Ventusa.

It was a few minutes after twelve when she saw him walking down the street, pushing through the crowd, a man different from all the others walking in the street. She frowned when she saw the pretty secretary with him. Marjorie hated this girl but she was helpless and could only hate all the others who seemed close to Robert Holton.

She pretended to be busy cleaning a table when they came in.

'Hello, Marjorie,' said Holton and he and Caroline came over to her table.

'Oh, hello, it's you again.' She smiled made herself sound matter-of-fact and bored, but her throat was suddenly full and she had to clear it before she could speak again. 'What you going to eat today?'

'I don't know,' said Holton and he and Caroline sat down at the table across from each other. 'What do you want, Caroline?'

'I'd like to see the menu, I think,' said Caroline in a voice that Marjorie Ventusa would like to have choked out of her.

'Here,' said Marjorie and she handed them two white menus.

They studied the menus.

Many people were coming in and going out of the restaurant. All the tables were full now and there were people standing and waiting for tables. Some of her customers were beginning to look at her, waiting for her to take their orders. She hoped Mrs Merrin would not notice how long she was taking with Robert Holton.

'I think,' said Caroline, frowning a thin hair-wide frown, 'I think I will have some tomato juice, and a lamb chop ...'

'No more lamb chops,' said Marjorie, trying to keep the triumph from her voice.

The hair-wide frown became a scowl. 'Then I'll have the veal.'

'Any vegetables?'

'Yes, the spinach.'

'You can have one other.'

'That's all.'

And Marjorie thought, 'the' spinach indeed. Why was it that when these people wanted to sound elegant they would talk about everything as 'the'?

'What do you want, Mr Holton?' She wished that she had the nerve to call him Bob, the right to call him that.

'Oh, I think I'll take the same.'

'Coffee, tea, or milk?' She said the words as though they were one word.

They both asked for coffee and Marjorie went quickly out of the dining-room and into the kitchen.

There was much more steam in the kitchen now than there had been at breakfast; as the day passed the kitchen got hotter, and steamier, and the cooks got more irritable and

59

Mrs Merrin more nervous and Marjorie Ventusa would become tired and sad.

She called the new orders to the cook. Then she picked up two small glasses of tomato juice and put them on her tray. She fingered one of them a moment, thinking that soon he would be drinking from it. She enjoyed thinking of this, though it only made her desire stronger and her sadness greater.

She didn't want to go back yet. She hoped Mrs Merrin would not come into the kitchen for a while.

But one of the swinging doors opened and Mrs Merrin walked into the kitchen. Quickly Marjorie picked up her tray and went back to the dining-room.

Caroline and Robert Holton were talking seriously and Marjorie, because of the noise of voices in the dining-room, couldn't hear what they were saying.

They stopped talking as she came up to them.

'Here you are,' said Marjorie Ventusa brightly, putting the glasses of tomato juice on the table.

Robert Holton smiled at her, showing his white even teeth.

'Have you got a date for tonight?' asked Robert Holton.

'You know I always do.'

'A sailor maybe?'

'I'm not saying.'

'Get one who'll take you to Italy.'

This was cruel but Marjorie smiled and forgave him. She had not been joking when they spoke of Italy. She did not think it fair of him to say this in front of the pretty girl, but Marjorie forgave him because he was young and because she felt about him in a certain way.

'Maybe we'll go to Capri together,' she said. 'Is it nice there?'

Holton nodded. 'Beautiful.'

Caroline said, 'I'm sure you don't want to take up any more of her time, Bob. She's got a lot of things to do.' Caroline gave Marjorie a brilliant smile. A man from the table next to theirs said loudly, 'When are you bringing me my soup?'

'In just a minute, sir.' Marjorie looked at Robert Holton once again, tried to catch his eye but he was talking now to Caroline and Marjorie Ventusa had been put quietly from his mind. She went back to the kitchen.

Outside the restaurant Richard Kuppelton and the receptionist Ruth were wondering whether anybody they knew would be in the restaurant; otherwise they would have to wait for a table.

Kuppelton looked through the window. He blinked nearsightedly. Then he saw Robert Holton and Caroline.

'Caroline's in there,' he said.

'With Bob?'

'Yes.'

'Well, let's go on in.' Ruth liked Robert Holton.

'Hello, hello,' said Kuppelton heartily when they were inside.

Caroline and Robert Holton appeared glad to see them.

'My gracious, it certainly is crowded,' said Ruth, pointing to the people standing.

'Lucky you people were here,' said Kuppelton.

'I don't,' said Ruth, 'see how the town stays so crowded all the time. I could understand it during the war but now . . . well, it's just impossible to go anywhere or do anything.'

'I know,' said Holton. 'Took me months to get a room.'

'Is it nice?' asked Caroline.

He shook his head. 'It's very depressing.'

'I guess I'm lucky to be living with my family,' said Kuppelton. 'It's real nice out where we are and there aren't so many people. I'd hate to have to live in the city.'

They talked of the places where they lived and then they started to talk of the places where they would like to live.

Kuppelton watched Holton as he talked and he tried to learn, by concentrating intensely, what he was thinking; to learn if Mr Murphy had said he would promote him. Holton's smooth forehead, however, was a wall and Kuppelton could not pierce it, could not discover the dreams behind it.

Marjorie came over to their table and put two plates of veal in front of Caroline and Robert. The veal was a uniform

tan colour, floating in a sea of red sauce. Two saucers of
dark-green spinach floating in water were put beside the
plates of veal.

'Looks good, doesn't it?' commented Marjorie.

'Sure, sure,' said Holton, looking at his plate with distaste.

Kuppelton ordered veal and Marjorie left.

Kuppelton looked at Ruth. She was dark, with a big nose
and with self-pitying eyes. Her complexion was oily and she
wore too much make-up. Ruth liked all men; she was sitting
very close to Robert Holton now.

'Any interesting people come into the office?' asked
Holton, turning to Ruth : as receptionist she was always able
to tell them about celebrities.

Ruth nodded. 'Laura Whitner was in to see Mr Heywood.'

Caroline was interested. 'She's the movie star, isn't she?'

Ruth nodded again, a birdlike motion. 'Why, she used
to be one of the biggest stars. I used to go see all her pictures.
My gracious, they were wonderful.'

Marjorie Ventusa returned with veal for Kuppelton and
the ham and eggs for Ruth.

'Oh, thank you,' said Ruth. 'I love ham,' she added.

Richard Kuppelton looked at Ruth with disapproval. She
was an aggressive woman and he was tired of aggressive
women. His mother was that way. Caroline was more what
he wanted. She had spirit but was not aggressive. There was
a difference between spirit and aggressiveness. He could not
quite define it but still there was a difference. Caroline could
act irritated with him and he would not mind. And she
always smiled, even when she was angry; he could not feel
that a woman who always smiled was aggressive. She had a
mind of her own but then he could handle that. Eating veal,
Richard Kuppelton felt he could handle anything.

Robert Holton finished eating. He sat back in his chair
and yawned.

'Bored?' asked Caroline.

He shook his head. 'No, not very. Just sleepy.'

'Well, I like that!' exclaimed Ruth. 'You'd think we
weren't good enough for him.' She said this in a way to let
him know she was being humorous.

62

Kuppelton decided, however, to develop what she'd said. 'Sure, he's a good friend of Mr Heywood.'

Ruth was impressed. 'I certainly wish I had your contacts then. I sure wouldn't be working in this lousy job.'

Robert Holton wanted to know what was wrong with her job.

'Oh, you know how it is. Doing the same thing day after day. It makes me sick. I'd like to do something exciting.'

'Like what?' asked Richard Kuppelton. This was his secret wish, too, but he would never have put it into words. He was delighted to hear someone else say it.

Ruth was not sure just what she wanted. She decided she would like to travel. Richard Kuppelton admitted, then, that he would like to travel. Caroline thought a moment and agreed with them that to travel would be the best thing anyone could do, the thing she wanted to do.

Robert Holton, who had travelled, said that he didn't care to leave New York again: not for many years at least.

'You're not adventurous,' said Caroline sadly.

Ruth protected him. 'After all, he's had some adventures. He was in the war.'

Richard Kuppelton was glad that Holton did not talk about the war. It made too great a difference between them and the women might have called attention to this difference.

He disliked Robert Holton because he was afraid of him. It was more than the threat to his job, much more than that. Caroline, whom Kuppelton wanted, seemed interested in him. He flattered himself that she was no more interested in Holton than she was in himself; still he was a threat.

Ruth was moving closer to Robert Holton now. Her thick curved lips, heavily painted a dark red, looked unpleasantly moist. Kuppelton had a desire to dry her mouth. He was amused, though, at the way she was playing up to Holton. She liked him now because of his influence, not because he was good-looking. Although Kuppelton, for one, couldn't see his handsomeness. Holton was well-built but not much better than he was; of course, Kuppelton had a slight stomach and

Holton didn't, but a few days of exercise and he could be as slim. He made a mental note to do some exercise.

Marjorie Ventusa arranged her hair in front of the steamy mirror. It didn't look too bad when she wore it over her ears. She pinned it back carefully. Perhaps she wouldn't have to get a snood after all.

She put some other people's orders on her tray and left the kitchen. The crowd waiting to be seated was beginning to thin and soon the lunch rush would be over.

She waited on the customers whose orders she had and then she moved over to the table where Robert Holton was sitting. He was very handsome, she thought. She looked at the others with him and she envied them all. They didn't understand what he was, how important he was.

The girl with blue eyes and slim legs she could not like. This was her rival — one of her rivals, anyway. She was glad that he never seemed particularly interested in this girl and for that matter the girl didn't seem interested in him. Still she was near, worked with him probably : she was a danger.

Then Marjorie Ventusa did not like the dark-haired girl with the big nose who sat close to him, but at least she was not a danger. She almost pitied this girl who had moved her chair so close to his that their legs were touching.

The other man was dull-looking and obviously interested in the girl with the blue eyes. Marjorie Ventusa wished him luck. Then, having thought these things about her customers, she walked over to their table.

'Ready for dessert?' asked Marjorie Ventusa cheerfully, trying not to look at Robert Holton.

They were ready.

Everyone decided to have vanilla ice-cream. Slowly she cleared the table. This was a hard thing to do, because she had to act as if she were in a hurry.

They talked at the table as though she weren't there. She was, naturally, used to that : she had been a waitress a long time, but today she was almost angry at being treated like a piece of furniture. She could do nothing about it, though. She picked up her tray and went into the kitchen.

64

Marjorie ordered the ice-cream. As she waited she wondered if there was any way she could ever see Robert Holton
in his other life. The mysteriously important life he had in
the brokerage firm. She tried to think of some way she could
get to know him in this other life. She could think of nothing.

The ice-cream was ready and she took it back to the
dining-room.

She gave them their dessert and only Holton said thank
you. She tried to expand this one phrase into a conversation
but it was too difficult. So she walked over to the next table
which was now empty. Slowly she placed dishes on her tray.
She was near enough to them to hear what they were saying.

Robert Holton was talking about his job : 'I don't mind
being in an office all day. I can't see why people mind that so
much.'

The dark girl with the big nose disagreed : 'It's much
more natural to be able to wander around like you want to
do. It's natural to travel, I think.'

He laughed. Marjorie liked his laugh. He said, 'You should
get married, that's what you should do.'

The dark girl became coquettish. 'But I haven't had any
offers yet. Of course, I'm open to any.'

The bitch, thought Marjorie Ventusa, disliking her now.

'You shouldn't have any trouble,' said Holton gallantly
and Marjorie like him for saying this.

'You're just saying that.'

Then the girl with the blue eyes and the dull man began
to talk together and their voices blended into the ocean-like
sound of many voices in the restaurant.

They finished the ice-cream.

Marjorie walked over to the table. 'Will there be anything
else?' she asked officially.

There was nothing else.

'We'll have our check please, Marjorie,' said Robert
Holton and she liked the way he said her name.

'Certainly.' She went to the cashier and had the four
checks totalled. Then she came back.

They paid her.

'Back to work,' said the blue-eyed girl with a sigh.

SEVEN

'Here we are,' said Caroline.

Ruth went to her desk in the reception room. 'I'll see you all later,' she said and she sat down and took out a large gold compact. Caroline watched her a moment as she powdered her nose, watched her with a certain pity because she was ugly.

'Come on,' said Kuppelton and he and Robert Holton walked on either side of her through the office. She was conscious of the envious stares of the other girls and she smiled at them as nicely as she could, knowing that they hated her for her smile.

Mr Murphy was not in the Statistical office. Everyone else was back, though. As she entered the room Caroline was conscious of a difference in the atmosphere. The women were quieter than usual and the men were watching. She looked and saw, sitting at Holton's desk, an army officer.

'Jim!' said Holton when he saw him; the other looked up.

'Hi,' he said and he got to his feet. They shook hands with Anglo-Saxon restraint, muttering monosyllables of greeting, each asking about the other's health.

Kuppelton went to his own desk without speaking to the army officer. Caroline stood expectantly beside Robert Holton, waiting to be introduced.

'This,' said Holton finally, 'is Caroline. Caroline, meet Jim Trebling.'

'How do you do,' said Trebling.

'How do you do,' said Caroline and they shook hands. His hand, she noticed, was rough and hard.

'You live in New York?' asked Caroline. This was always

a good beginning because it could lead to all sorts of confessions.

He shook his head. 'No, I'm from California. I'm from Los Angeles.'

She was impressed. 'That's where Hollywood is isn't it? You from Hollywood?'

No, he was not from Hollywood. He lived nearby.

'I'd certainly like to visit out there.'

'It's not as interesting as New York.'

She gave a little laugh to show her scorn for New York, her laugh levelling the buildings and cracking Grant's Tomb. 'It's awful here,' she said. 'We have an awful climate.'

He raised the buildings again. 'Oh, I think it's pretty exciting. You've got so many things. This is really the first time I've seen New York. Bob and I went overseas from here and we came back here but I never really saw the town.'

'Are you regular army?' she asked. Men in uniform were becoming rare.

'No, I'm getting out soon. I signed up for a little while longer.'

'Oh.'

He and Robert Holton began to talk then about the army and she felt shut out. She stood there wondering whether she should go or not. She rather liked this young man. He was a lieutenant, at least he had one bar on his shoulder and she thought that lieutenants wore a single bar: the war had been such a long time ago and she had forgotten so many things.

He had dark eyes and bleached-looking hair which Caroline had always found attractive in men. His skin was rather pale for a Californian; all Californians had brown skin in her imagination. He was not particularly handsome, though he looked rather distinguished, with sharp features and circles under his eyes.

'Are you in the East long?' she asked.

He looked at her as if he had forgotten she was there; still, he was very polite. 'No, I'm only here for a week.'

'Looking around?'

'Yes, looking around.'

67

'Caroline,' said Robert Holton, as though explaining an important thing, 'Caroline is the belle of the office.'

'I can see that,' said Trebling without too much effort, saying it almost naturally, a hard thing to do.

'Oh, thank you,' said Caroline. Now she didn't know what to say. She looked at his ribbons. She counted them mechanically, the way she did before the war ended : five ribbons. 'You must've been around quite a bit,' she said finally, speaking before the silence her last words had made became another conversation.

Trebling nodded seriously. 'Yes, I saw quite a bit. No more than Bob did, though.'

'That must've been nice,' said Caroline, 'your being able to serve together everywhere.'

'Yes, it was.'

She knew that they were waiting for her to go but she wasn't ready yet. 'Do you like being in the army in peacetime?'

'No, not particularly.'

'Well, you'll be out soon, I suppose.'

'Quite soon.'

She had to go now. She couldn't understand what kept her standing there foolishly trying to make a conversation by herself. It was not as if Lieutenant Trebling were handsome or unusual.

Caroline made her great effort. 'Well,' she said, 'I guess I'll see you later, Mr Trebling.' Was that the right name? She wasn't sure. She hoped she hadn't said it wrong.

'Nice to have met you, Caroline.' She smiled at him, her face at a three-quarter angle : her most flattering angle. Then, with great nonchalance, she walked slowly back to her desk.

Trebling was surprised at the way Holton looked out of uniform.

To have lived several years with a person who looked always one way and then to see him later another way is startling. Jim Trebling had always thought of Holton as a soldier : he could not get used to him as a civilian in an office.

'Sit down, Jim.' Holton pointed to a chair beside his desk. They both sat down. Trebling felt a little awkward. The office was too formal for him and he was not at ease.

Jim looked at Holton, trying to get accustomed to him. 'You've certainly changed. I don't know if I'd have recognized you.'

Robert Holton laughed a little self-consciously. 'These civilian clothes *are* different. They make you feel different.'

'You're really settling down, I guess.'

'I'm afraid so.'

'I wish I could. Maybe I will when I get out . . . I don't know.'

'What do you think you're going to do?'

Jim shrugged. 'I don't know. I've been thinking of starting some kind of a business. You know, what we used to talk about before you got out.'

Holton nodded. 'That's a good idea, I guess. I thought of it, too, but of course the odds are against you.'

Trebling was surprised to hear Holton say this. 'I know it,' he said.

Holton saw then that he hadn't said the right thing. He tried to explain. 'I don't mean you shouldn't start a business. I just mean something might go wrong.' He was saying worse things now; he stopped.

Jim changed the subject. 'How do you like being out?'

'Oh, it's pretty wonderful. Just to be able to stay in one place . . .'

'I guess it's nice for a while.'

Holton sighed. 'I don't think I'll ever travel again.'

Jim was surprised. 'I thought you were going to go around the world. Don't you remember when we used to talk about seeing more of Italy?'

'Well, maybe sometime. I hadn't stopped moving for very long then.'

'No, that's right, you hadn't. As they talked Jim Trebling became more uneasy. This was a person he had not met before and he was surprised and sorry. Robert Holton had been different as a soldier.

As they talked, the words forming conventional patterns

69

and hiding their real thoughts, Jim thought of the war.

'You remember the time we were in Florence?'

Holton said that he remembered it very well.

They spoke then of Florence and as they talked Jim Trebling began to remember many things.

The city had been liberated for several months. The war was almost over and Holton and Trebling were able to take a week's leave; they went to Florence.

Parts of the city had been badly damaged. The old buildings on the Arno had been levelled in many places but the Ponte Vecchio was still there. These things had not been very important, however, because they had not gone to see antiques. They had gone to rest, to meet women and to try to find enough liquor to get drunk on.

They stayed with a family outside of the town; they stayed in a place called Fiesole.

Trebling remembered the house clearly : long and rambling, dirty-white stucco with small iron balconies beneath the larger windows. A rock garden, dusty grey-green olive trees and an unearthly view of the valley in which was Florence.

The house belonged to a family named Bruno, friends of Robert Holton's mother. They had invited the two of them to stay as long as they liked : in those days it was a good policy to have American soldiers in one's home.

Robert Holton had liked a girl named Carla. Trebling had liked her too, but not as much as Holton did. He remembered one night when the three had sat on the terrace, watching the city.

It was summer and the night was warm and vibrant. The city lights glittered in the valley-cup; the lights were golden and flickering and the river shone darkly.

They sat on a stone ledge, their feet dangling above the rock garden. Carla was between them; her hair was dark and her face pale. They sat like this, watching the lights of the city and listening to the sound of insects whirring in the night.

And Jim had said, embarrassed by the long silence, 'It's so peaceful here.'

The other two acted as if they had not heard him. Holton, sitting close beside Carla, touched her.

And then she had said, 'It seems like such a long time ago.' They thought of this as they sat in the blue darkness.

Holton finally spoke, saying. 'Isn't it a shame that this has to change again?'

They had been surprised to hear him say this; Trebling was more surprised than Carla because, though he had known Holton longer, she knew him better. Trebling was surprised to hear Holton speak seriously : he was never serious at other times. He always tried to be funny.

'Why *should* this change again?' asked Carla, looking at him, trying to tell his expression in the dark.

Holton only sighed and said, 'Because everything changes when you go away.'

'You can come back,' said Carla and Jim remembered now the exact way she had said that and he was sorry for her.

Holton didn't answer for a moment and then he had said, 'Yes, I suppose you can.' They knew then that he would not come back and Trebling could sense her sadness as they watched the lights flickering below them.

'Do you remember Carla?' asked Jim suddenly, his mind adjusting to the present.

'The girl in Florence? Sure, I remember her. Was that her name . . . Carla?'

'That's right.'

'She was very nice looking, wasn't she?'

'Yes.'

'Sure, I remember her.'

'I thought you liked her quite a bit,' said Trebling, not looking at Holton.

'I suppose I did. We ran into a lot of people, though. There were so many people.'

Trebling agreed that there had been a number of people in Europe, people they had known.

'That was a good town, Florence,' said Holton suddenly. 'It was.'

'We were there a week, weren't we?'

Holton nodded, and Trebling watched him to see how he felt; Holton's face told him nothing, though. He was only remembering.

'It's certainly a nice feeling to be out,' said Holton finally.

'I guess it must be.'

'Not having to worry about being moved from place to place.'

They were standing in the Roman Forum. All around them were pieces of shattered marble, shattered in earlier wars. Trebling and Holton had looked at three slender columns of marble, all that was left of a temple.

Trebling had remarked, 'I'll bet those pillars are pretty old.'

Holton agreed, 'Maybe a thousand years old.'

Together they had looked at the three columns of the ruined temple.

Trebling asked, 'Do you think you would've ever got here except in the army?'

'No. I don't guess so.'

'I probably wouldn't have either.'

'It's sort of interesting.'

And Trebling had said, 'I like the travelling part of all this.'

Robert Holton agreed to this and then they began to complain about other things.

Trebling sat back in his chair and looked around the office. He didn't like offices and he didn't like this one at all. The clear constant light standardized the people in the room.

'How do you like it here?' he asked.

Holton shrugged. 'O.K., I suppose. It's something to do.'

'You think you'll stay in this sort of work?'

'Probably, I don't know yet.'

'I had thought you might go into this new thing with me.'

'Well...'

Neither spoke for a moment.

Finally Trebling asked, 'Can I smoke in here?'

'I'm sorry, Jim, but . . .'

'Sure, I know : rules.'

'I'm sorry. These people are awful stiff about a lot of things.'

Jim Trebling wished again that he hadn't come. He had an impulse to run away. 'What're you doing tonight?' he asked finally.

'I'm going to a big cocktail party.'

'Being social, eh?'

'Well, you know you have to make contacts . . .' he continued, explaining himself carefully.

Then Holton asked Jim about himself, and he listened as Jim talked. The cataloguing of army camps, the different duties in each, the girl he had decided to marry and then didn't, his current leave of absence, the trip across the country, the pleasure of seeing Robert Holton again.

Trebling told this story automatically, as one always tells a much-told personal story and as he told this he wondered what had happened to Holton.

In the war he had been considered wild. He had spent most of the time laughing at things. He had been easily bored and now he was changed.

'It must be nice to be out,' Trebling repeated, not knowing what else to say.

And Robert Holton explained to him in detail why it was so nice to be free.

Paris had been the most interesting place of all. They had spent two days there. Trebling had been very conscientious and had insisted that they see places and landmarks and they had actually tried to see a few but then Holton decided that there was not enough time for that. They met two girls. Trebling could not remember their names; he could remember nothing about them except that they were rather pretty and claimed to be sisters.

The girls had suggested they go on a picnic. Holton had liked this idea and he managed to get some food from the mess officer of a near-by company. They took bicycles and drove out of Paris. They rode through Sèvres and some small towns on the outskirts. They approached Versailles but the girls didn't care to go into the town and so they turned left from the main road. At a small town called Jouy-en-Josas they stopped, and on the dark green lawn of a bombed-out château they had their picnic.

The sky was overcast that day. And the woods that surrounded the château were blue and smoky and looked mysterious, like the pictures of enchanted forests in children's books.

When they had finished lunch Holton wanted to go walk in the woods. Only one of the girls spoke English.

'Let's take a walk in the woods,' Holton suggested.

The two girls giggled and talked together very quickly in French. The one who spoke English finally said, 'Sure, we go walk in the woods with you.' They walked in the woods.

Hand in hand the two couples walked between the misty trees. There was no underbrush here and the trees came up out of the stony, grass-covered ground, free and straight.

The two girls understood what was expected of them. His most vivid memory was not of the one he had but of Holton's: a stocky pink-faced girl. He remembered clearly the way her head lolled against the tree, her eyes closed and her thick lips slightly ajar. He remembered that her hair was almost the same colour as the bark of the tree.

'Say, Bob, do you remember those two girls from Paris?'

'When was that?'

'You know, the time we spent on the picnic.'

'I'm afraid I've forgotten.' That was that.

A large important-looking man came into the office. When he saw Trebling with Holton he stopped in the middle of the room, changed his course with the unself-conscious dignity of a schooner under full sail, and walked straight over to them.

Holton got to his feet quickly and Trebling did the same, sensing that this was a person of importance.

'Jim Trebling, this is Mr Murphy, the Chief of our section.'

'Glad to meet you, Lieutenant.' They shook hands

74

vigorously, Mr Murphy smiling with goodwill.

'Well, Lieutenant, I suppose you'll be getting out soon?'

Mechanically Trebling explained what he was planning to do.

'Think you'll go into Business?' asked Mr Murphy.

'Maybe, I don't know.'

'Lot of openings now for a young man who wants to get ahead.'

'There probably are.'

They talked for a while of Business as though it were a state of being.

Trebling looked at Holton as Mr Murphy talked, looked at him, trying to find something familiar in his face. For a moment as he looked he thought he could see a tightness about the mouth, an effort at control but Jim Trebling could not tell what Holton was controlling and the mouth soon relaxed and he could tell nothing then.

Coming back on the boat together they had talked of what they were going to do when they got out.

'I think I'd like to make money,' said Holton looking at the white wake of the ship.

'That's not a bad idea. How?'

'Damned if I know.'

'We could always start that pottery business I was telling you about, back in California.'

'That's a thought.'

'Of course there's a lot of other things we could do.'

'I suppose it's all a matter of picking the right one.'

They looked at the grey water and thought of new things, of works not yet begun. Pensively Holton leaned out over the railing and spat. Trebling, interested, did the same. For several moments they were in serious contest to determine who could spit the farthest. Holton won, although Trebling claimed he had been helped by a gust of wind.

Then they walked about the decks of the transport. Soldiers were everywhere. They sat in groups on the covered hatches, they leaned over the railings to look at the sea and, also, to be sick.

'I guess all these people are going to be trying the same thing,' said Holton suddenly.

'Try what? Starting a business?'

'Sure.'

'I don't think so.'

'A lot of them will.'

'So what?'

'I guess it could work.' They stopped amidships and looked out to sea again. 'I'd certainly like to have a lot of money,' said Holton sincerely.

'So would I,' said Trebling with casual sincerity.

They had decided then to start in together when they got out of the army. Holton had been discharged first, however, and he had immediately joined Heywood and Golden. In his occasional letters Holton never mentioned the business again. Trebling remembered that now and was sorry so much had changed.

Mr Murphy was talking about Business.

Holton was listening to him with what appeared to be interest. Trebling shook himself and tried to act as if he had been following the lesson Mr Murphy had been giving him.

'Very nice to have met you, Lieutenant,' said Mr Murphy at last.

'Nice to meet you.' They shook hands. Mr Murphy turned to Holton. 'I'd like to see you for a moment if your friend doesn't mind.'

'Certainly.' Holton gestured to Trebling to stay where he was. Then Mr Murphy and Holton went over to the other end of the office where the windows were.

Jim Trebling sat in his uncomfortable chair beneath the fluorescent lights. He wanted to leave this office, leave it now and not come back. He couldn't understand Holton any longer. He no longer knew him.

Trebling was aware of someone standing beside him. He looked up : it was the blue-eyed girl. He started to get to his feet.

'Don't move,' she said. 'I'm just passing by. Mr Murphy and Bob seemed to be having some sort of conference. I thought I'd wait outside the gate till they were through.'

'Sit down,' said Trebling.

'Thank you.' She sat down in the chair beside him. He wondered what to say to her, what to talk about.

'Have you been here long?' he asked.

She told him that she had been there for several years.

'It must be interesting working in a place like this.'

She laughed. 'It's pretty awful, I think. As jobs go, of course, it's not bad.'

'But you'd rather not work at all.'

'That's right.'

'Well, you'll probably be married soon.' This was a leading question. There was a simple ritual to conversation with pretty girls who might be had.

She recognized this and answered according to the ritual, 'Oh, maybe someday, when I meet the right person.'

This could mean a lot. He was interested now. 'That's important, meeting the right person.'

They were both silent, thinking how important it was to meet the right person.

Trebling began to think of this girl (was her name Caroline?) quite seriously. It was such an important thing to discover : if she could be had or not. For one night she might be very pleasant. He liked the way she looked. But then he thought of certain other one-night stands and of the phone calls and letters and emotion that often came of them. He would be very careful about this. He resumed.

'I suppose you can have a pretty good time in New York if you know the right places to go.'

'Yes, there are some nice places. You have to be very careful, though.'

'A lot of them are clip joints, I guess.'

She laughed. 'I'll say they are.'

'Depends, I guess, on who you go out with.'

'Well, you should know your way around.'

They were drawing nearer and nearer to the act. Everything was going well. She was returning all his signals. He began to breathe a little hard as they approached the gateway.

'I know so few people in New York,' he said. 'Bob's really the only person I know well. I don't know any girls.'

'Well, there's a lot of them around.'

'I know.' He paused and then he began to speak carefully but casually. 'I was going out tonight but I don't think I will now.'

'Why?'

'It's not much fun alone.' This was said almost pathetically.

'What about Bob?'

'He's going to that cocktail party.'

'Oh, yes, I forgot.' A pause now, a silence with great meaning in it.

'Maybe,' and he was saying it at last, 'maybe *you* might go out with me tonight.'

'Me!' Surprised, pleasure, a certain asperity, all these emotions splendidly portrayed in that one word. 'Well . . .'

'Of course if you're busy . . .'

'Oh, no . . .' She spoke almost too quickly. 'I'm not really certain,' she added, regaining her dignity. 'Perhaps you might call me back around five. I'll know then.' At that moment both of them knew.

'That would be fine. I hope you don't think it's . . .'

'Certainly not.' Then she said that any friend of Bob's was a friend of hers.

Trebling felt pleased with himself for having managed so well. It might take a week but it would still be pleasant. He looked forward to the final moment of yielding. He sighed and started to think of other things.

Caroline, seeing that Holton was on his way back, got up from her chair. 'Nice to have seen you, Lieutenant. I'll be looking forward to your call.'

He also stood up. 'I hope you can make it.' She said that she did, too, and they both knew what was going to happen. Robert Holton came back and Caroline left.

'That's a pretty girl,' said Trebling.

'Caroline? Yes, she's pretty nice.'

They stood looking at each other awkwardly. 'Shall we get together tomorrow evening?' suggested Holton.

'Sure, that'd be fine.'

'Well, listen, Jim, it's been wonderful seeing you . . .'

'And I've enjoyed it . . .' Their voices intermingled into a single sound. Neither of them listened to the words of the other.

'See you tomorrow then, Bob?'

'See you then.' They said good-bye and Jim Trebling left the office. As he stood in the reception room waiting for the elevator he felt sad the way Holton had changed. It was such a shame because they had once been very close. Then Jim Trebling thought of Caroline and he felt happier. The Carolines were the important things.

The elevator door opened and he stepped inside.

EIGHT

At five-thirty the world ceased to be official and became private.

Happily Robert Holton put away his books and figures and prepared to leave. Monday was over and he wouldn't let himself think of the other days of his week.

Caroline was putting on her hat and Mr Murphy sat at his desk behind her, dreaming, his eyes fixed shrewdly upon nothing.

Robert Holton walked over to Caroline.

'Ready to go?'

She nodded. 'All ready.' Together they walked through the emptying offices, rode down the crowded elevator, and stepped out into the more crowded street.

The sky was grey now and the sun had vanished behind buildings. The air was cool and the smell of exhaust was strong as cars moving slowly in the streets, trying to escape to less crowded places. They walked with the stream of people towards the subway opening. They talked.

'Guess what?' said Caroline.

'What?'

'I'm going out tonight.'

'Well?'

'I'm going out with Lieutenant Trebling.'

He was surprised. 'That was fast work. Did he do that while he was in the office?'

'We talked about it. He called me back later and I told him I'd go out with him.'

'Well, well.' Holton was admiring but Caroline was not sure whether he was admiring her or Trebling.

'I think he's nice,' she said, not committing herself.

'Yes, he's a good guy.'

They crossed the street nervously and in silence. On the other side they went on talking.

'Tell me something about him?' she asked.

'There's not much to tell. He's from the West Coast. He went to UCLA, I think, and his old man's in the insurance business. He went into the army about the same time I did and he's still in.'

'That's not what I want to know.'

'Well, what do you want to know?'

She had trouble saying this. 'Oh, you know . . . the sort of person he is. All that sort of thing.'

Robert Holton, who hadn't thought much about it, had a hard time answering. 'I guess he's what you'd call a dreamer. He's not very practical. He always wants to start things . . . businesses, you know. In the war he was pretty good and other people liked him. He wasn't very wild then.'

'Is he now?'

'Just his ideas. In those days I used to be the wild one.'

She laughed and thought he was joking with her and this made him angry and sad but there was nothing he could do about it because he had assumed a certain identity with her and it had to be maintained.

'I'll bet you were wild!'

'We all change,' he said.

She wasn't interested in how he'd changed, though : she was interested in Jim Trebling. 'I don't suppose he's engaged or anything like that?' She was casual.

Holton laughed. 'No, you can get him if you want to.'

'I didn't mean that at all. What do you mean by saying that?'

'Not a thing.'

She went on talking for several moments, trying to be indignant. Then they crossed another street and she stopped talking.

They walked with the current of people, walked uncomfortably but deliberately over the sidewalk ventilators of the subway beneath. As they walked they could feel the thunder of a subway train under their feet, vibrating upward, like a great emotion, into their stomachs.

Then they came to the opening of the subway. With a deep breath they descended into the pit. Like lemmings dashing seaward the people pushed down the steps and into already crowded trains.

Caroline and Holton were separated. A sudden push of the crowd threw her into the train just before the door closed. He caught a last glimpse of her serene beauty being crushed between a large Negress and a tall white man. The train gave a rumble and pulled away.

Holton stood on the concrete platform with a hundred others who missed this train and were waiting for the next.

He walked up and down between the concrete pillars, looking at the broken machines which were supposed to sell gum and peanuts and, from habit, he put his fingers into one of the slots to see if anything was there : nothing was there however.

He admired the advertisements. His favourite one, the girl advertising beer, was not in this station but there were others. Two very excellent ones of movie actresses, young woman hauntingly attractive with red lips. He admired these even though the most beautiful actress of all had her front teeth blacked out and a crude phallic image drawn over her passionate face. There were people in the world who would do those things, of course, and he was not annoyed.

The other advertisements were less interesting and he didn't look at them very long.

Another train roared through the tunnel, stopping with great noise; the doors opened and people flowed out; then another rush to get on the train. Robert Holton allowed himself to be carried into the hot stale car.

He liked to walk in the Park. In the evenings the Park was the most peaceful place in the city. A few people would be sitting on the benches and a few couples would be walking between trees but there were never many people here in the early evening and the ones that were there were always quiet.

As Robert Holton walked the miracle of the street lamps

took place, white light filling the bulbs and changing the early evening, the twilight period, to a premature night.

He walked quickly now because it was almost six o'clock. Mrs Raymond Stevanson's cocktail parties often went on until nine or ten o'clock and occasionally they lasted all night but he couldn't know this for certain and he didn't want to be late.

Robert Holton thought sadly about Jim Trebling as he walked, breathing the cool air. A short time had made a lot of difference and he was aware of this difference.

Trebling was apt to be impractical. It was a likeable quality in the army; he himself hadn't made much sense in those days, but things had changed now. This was the time to be practical and Jim Trebling was not.

A couple were embracing beside a large rock. He watched them with interest as he went by.

He had tried to pretend to be the same but the effort, or the change, had been too great. It made him unhappy to think that he and Trebling had really been so different, had always been so different, even in those days. He was shocked to think that Trebling remembered the army as a pleasant period of his life. There had been times, of course . . .

Another couple came out of the woods, walked to the pathway and looked uncertainly about them, as though unsure of themselves. When he glanced at them they looked at him angrily, as if he had been spying. He walked away.

Robert Holton was not sure why he had changed towards Trebling. He wanted to be the same. He wanted to take up the friendship where it had been broken but he could not. He was not going to change again.

A nurse with a baby carriage was hurrying streetward. It was late, probably much too late for her to be out with the baby. As she passed him he caught a glimpse of the child and saw that it was staring vacantly ahead, concentrating upon growth.

He followed the nurse and the carriage towards the street. Robert Holton smiled to himself when he thought of Caroline and Jim Trebling going out together. It was always interesting when people out of different periods of his life

83

came to know each other. He had never associated Trebling
with Caroline before.

He took a last deep breath of air before he left the Park.
He wished vaguely that he might have more time to walk in
the Park and straighten out certain things.

The uptown streets were not crowded. A few people were
coming home from work; most of the people were already
home by now. Children played together in the streets, shout-
ing at one another in sharp hoarse voices. A smell of cooking
was in the streets.

There was no mail for him.

This was not a good day. On the good days there was mail;
days could be bad when there wasn't any. Not that there was
anyone Robert Holton wanted to hear from in particular but
he was less alone when he had letters to read.

'Been a nice day,' said the person behind the desk.

'It certainly has,' said Robert Holton.

'Won't be long until it's winter,' said the person behind
the desk.

'It won't be long,' said Holton. He turned then and
walked through the dingy lobby to the elevator.

He and the elevator boy discussed the kind of day it had
been. They also decided that it would be winter soon.

His room looked no more cheerful than usual. Robert
Holton sat down on the bed, leaving the room dark. It gave
him a feeling of power to think that, when he chose, he
could turn on a light and dispel the darkness.

He started to think of Trebling but stopped himself. There
was nothing to be done now. The old friendship was gone.

Trebling had mentioned a girl named Carla. He remembered her well. She had been pretty and intense and wealthy.
He had not thought about her for a long time. She had been
a strange girl, gentle and understanding. He had been greatly
attracted to her and she to him.

They had walked around Florence and Fiesole. She had
taken him to old palaces and churches although he hadn't
wanted to go. When he had objected she told him that she
was trying to show him something. He never knew what it

84

was she wanted to show him. When he left Florence he told her that he would write : he didn't, though, and he had not thought of her again until today.

The thing he had liked most about Carla, the thing he could remember now, was her way of understanding him. She once told him that it wasn't necessary to finish sentences when they talked; that she knew what he would say and that he should know what she would say.

Sitting in the dark of his hotel room, Robert Holton thought of all the women he had known and liked; some he had slept with and some he hadn't. Most of them he had forgotten. Now he only thought of them when someone else recalled them to him.

And he did remember about Paris. He remembered the picnic outside Versailles, although he could not remember the faces of the two girls.

In Europe there had been so many women. He often was surprised now when he thought of how many he had known. There were periods when he had been never satisfied. Both Trebling and he had gone about it like hunters. Trebling was probably still hunting, thought Holton suddenly, and he wondered if he was, too. No, that was behind him. He had to live and act in a different way now. He had to be a different person.

Robert Holton turned on the light beside his bed. He blinked in the yellow light and suddenly he was dissatisfied with the room. He wished for the first time that he were somewhere else; it didn't matter where, just somewhere else. He was a person of great logic, though, and he asked himself what he would rather be doing and he couldn't think of anything else to do. He didn't want to travel. He had no desire to escape. There was no place to escape to anyway and Robert Holton who had a kind of wisdom knew that.

Then he took his clothes off and got under the shower. This was usually the happiest part of his day. The warm water gave him a feeling of security, relaxing him, the world fell into a genial perspective. He finished bathing reluctantly and dressed quickly.

Finally he stood in front of the mirror again and combed

his hair. He was glad to see that he wasn't losing his hair. Sometimes he thought he was; at other times he knew he wasn't.

He wasn't displeased with himself. He wasn't pleased either but he knew that he was acceptable. There was no use in worrying, anyway. He wished sometimes that his nose could have been more aquiline. He would like to look more impressive. Perhaps his face would get that way as he grew older. He turned away from the mirror.

He looked at the picture on the wall and wondered for the hundredth time why the painter had made everything look so blue. The painter had made one of the apples almost sky-blue and Robert Holton had never seen an apple that colour before and he found it hard to believe that there was much advantage in so misrepresenting things. Perhaps in certain parts of France the apples were blue.

He was dressed and ready now. He looked at his watch and saw that it was a quarter to seven : he would have to hurry. Robert Holton looked around the room to see if there was anything he wanted to take with him. There wasn't. He put on his trench coat, turned out the light, and left the room.

The elevator boy wanted to know if he was going to a party.

'Sure, I'm going to a big party.'

'Lots of girls, I bet.' The pale thin elevator boy was interested.

'A whole lot of them.'

'Boy, I wish I was going out to something like that. This night work is getting me down. I ain't getting much relaxation.' He winked to show what he meant by relaxation and Holton smiled sympathetically.

Robert Holton stopped by the desk.

'I'll be back pretty early,' he said to the clerk. He always told them when to expect him, told them from force of habit because no one ever wanted to know.

'Yes, sir,' said the clerk. 'Nice night tonight,' he added.

'Nice autumn night,' agreed Robert Holton.

They discussed the evening politely. Then Robert Holton left the hotel.

It was darker now and cooler. The night was refreshing and he felt suddenly strong and contented. The depression of the office left him and he was becoming alive. He prepared himself for the party and for the evening ahead. He walked briskly down the street and, to emphasize his mood of sudden power, he hailed a taxi and rode in it happily, without regret for the money he was spending.

2
NIGHT

NINE

The party seemed to be going well. Although Mrs Raymond Stevanson hated cocktail parties, finding her own almost as bad as other people's, she still felt she had to give them and she worked very hard to make them outstanding.

Several hundred well-dressed people wandered about her large apartment, looking at the furniture, each other, and the five different paintings of Mrs Stevanson. There were no traces of Mr Stevanson in the apartment. He had died early in her career, leaving her his money and four race horses. She had sold the horses and she had saved quite a bit of the money. Now at fifty-five, she was a famous hostess and somewhat overweight.

'Good evening, Helena.' Mrs Stevanson turned around and saw the thin malicious face of Beatrice Jordan. They were contemporaries.

'Beatrice! How marvellous!' They touched cheeks with slight frowns, then came apart again with affectionate smiles.

Beatrice stood back a moment and looked at Mrs Stevanson. Beatrice was extremely nearsighted but much too vain to wear glasses. To see clearly she was forced to tuck her chin down and look upward, a habit which had given her an undeserved reputation as a coquette. She did this now.

'Helena, you've lost weight! How?'

Mrs Stevanson was pleased. 'Does it really show?' She patted her cement-hard corseted buttock.

'Not so much around there,' said Beatrice, thinking for a moment. 'More around here.' She touched her own meagre breasts.

'You think so?' Mrs Stevanson was irritated and angry

91

with herself for allowing Beatrice Jordan to say such a thing. Mrs Stevanson was proud of her breasts. Several of the famous painters had called her voluptuous.

'It's been lovely seeing you, Helena darling. I've got to join my escort now. I came with Clyde.'

Beatrice said this triumphantly but gained no victory.

'You came with Clyde. How wonderful! I'm dining with him tomorrow.'

'Indeed?'

'Is he here now?'

'He's in the other room.'

'Do tell him to see me before he leaves. There are *so* many people here.'

'I will, darling. Lovely to see you.' Beatrice smiled, showing her artful white false teeth and Mrs Stevanson smiled back showing her own artful white false teeth. The two women parted.

Mrs Stevanson was annoyed but she had found that the older she got the less interested she was in what people said. It was well known anyway that Beatrice Jordan was a cat.

Mrs Stevanson walked now from group to group. The groups unfolded for her like flowers before the sun. She would disappear for a moment into the heart of one and then it would unfold again, release her and become tight and compact once more.

Certain groups contained people more important than other groups. In these she lingered longest, smiling the most attractive, saying her superlatives.

In the dining-room a buffet had been set on a long table. Three footmen (hired for the evening only) guarded it from the hungry-looking guests, betrayed it to the superior ones who were not hungry.

Twenty or thirty people were gathered here and they looked rather self-conscious as she approached. Somehow everyone felt rather guilty to be caught eating heavily (they *were* eating heavily, she noticed) at a cocktail party.

She moved heartily about the dining-room, demanding that they eat more, suggesting they try something they had not already tried. And then, to show she was mortal, she ate a piece of white bread with Virginia ham on it.

The dining-room under control, Mrs Stevanson marched back through the drawing-room, accepted greetings and homage with a tiny smile that one of her lovers (he was dead now) had said reminded him of La Gioconda.

Mrs Stevanson, among other things, believed in art. To-night she had invited several writers, a few painters, one sculptor whose name she couldn't remember, and a half-dozen actors whose names everyone knew.

She had also invited George *Robert* Lewis. For some obscure reason his middle name was always gallicized, legiti-matizing the Lewis. He had been born and raised in Alabama. Unfortunately for his family he had very early shown a passion for the artistic as well as a marked tendency towards Socratic love. When he decided that the thing he most wanted was to go to Paris and become an artist, his family did not object; in fact, his father had suggested that if he wanted to live the rest of his life in Paris it was all right with him. Lewis lived there in the Nineteen-Thirties. He returned in the Forties.

Mrs Stevanson thought him cute and she was in the habit of telling her friends that, although his habits were shocking, he was still, quite charming and so *advanced*. And then he was marvellously decadent and the decadent was becoming popular now that the artificial virility of war was safely past.

George *Robert* Lewis was also an interesting person to know because he was the editor of *Regarde*, a magazine which had been called *avant garde* before that phrase be-came old-fashioned. Under his editorship the magazine had advanced all new things in the hope that one of the new things thus championed would be a success. So far none had but he still was championing and, though Mrs Stevanson seldom understood a word he said, she felt he was awfully brave to say the dreadful things he did about people and morals, especially people.

Lewis was talking to a small brown man whom she didn't remember inviting.

'Dear Helena,' said Lewis as she approached, 'you look wonderfully well-preserved.'

93

'George, you're a devil,' said Mrs Stevanson, secretly pleased.

Lewis embraced her in much the same way Beatrice Jordan had. 'What mad things have you been doing, Helena? Something naughty, I'm sure.' His innocent blue eyes sparkled as he spoke. He had the expressions of a child.

'Nothing that you couldn't equal. It was delightful of you to come.'

'I was so bored, darling, I felt that if I stayed home another moment I should go completely out of my mind.'

'Poor thing.' They talked this way with each other, talked with the casual rudeness of people who have met each other at many parties. He was an amazing person, thought Mrs Stevanson, looking at him carefully. He was slim and not very tall, with a pretty feminine face and, except for the small bitter lines about his mouth, he looked as if he were still in his twenties. His actual age was unknown. Mrs Stevanson thought he was forty.

'And whom have we here?' asked Mrs Stevanson, turning to face the small brown man beside him, a social smile on her face.

'Why, don't you know . . . this is . . .' He said the name quickly. It was something foreign and difficult. She would have to call Lewis up the next day and ask him. She shook hands with the little man and saw that he was impressed with her. She smiled as George *Robert* Lewis explained him. He was a Greek and a professor and he knew a lot about poetry.

'*But* Helena, he has the most fabulous philosophy. I really think it's never been done before. What was it again, Timon?' Mrs Stevanson knew his first name now.

'I'm sure Mrs Stevanson wouldn't be interested.' As a matter of fact Mrs Stevanson wasn't interested but she encouraged him.

'I should love to know,' she said. How like an earthenware pot he looks, she thought as he began to tell her his theory.

'You see it is based on the legend of the Golden Fleece. I have substituted the artistic ultimate in place of the fleece and, to carry the myth to its final parallel, I envisage all artists as travelling upon an Argosy . . .' She listened, politely,

94

carefully to the sound of the words, ignoring their meanings. She glanced up and down the large white-panelled room. No one was drunk.

'Isn't it stimulating?' asked Lewis when the Greek named Timon had finished.

'Wonderful,' murmured Mrs Stevanson.

The Greek flushed happily. 'I don't think the Argosy's ever been interpreted quite that way before.'

'I'm sure it hasn't,' agreed Mrs Stevanson. She was becoming impatient now. Her own Argosy would have to begin again. More guests were arriving.

'Have you seen the new ballet?' asked Lewis suddenly.

'No, I haven't seemed to have had the time.'

'It's dreadful. But the boy . . .' Lewis made little motions with his hand, with his mouth, with his body. His eyes glittered their blue innocence, their cheerful pleasure. He described the boy to her and in great detail he told her how he was going to arrange a meeting.

'You're too clever to stay alive, my pet,' said Mrs Stevanson. She hoped that none of her other guests were overhearing this. Most of them were quite worldly but a few weren't and it would never do to have them hear him.

'I must . . .' began Mrs Stevanson moving slowly away.

'So nice to have met you,' said the small Greek named Timon.

'The pleasure . . .' murmured Mrs Stevanson.

Lewis waved to her. 'I shall see you later, Helena.' Mrs Stevanson wondered irritably why fairies had to have such unpleasant voices.

Several new arrivals were in the foyer. She recognized Mr Heywood immediately. He was passively allowing one of the footmen to take his overcoat away from him.

'Heywood dear, it was so nice of you to come.'

'It's nice to be here, Helena.' He looked unhappily at the footman, retreating with the overcoat.

'And where is your lovely wife?' Mrs Stevanson knew perfectly well they were no longer on speaking terms.

'My wife?' Heywood became dreamy, vague and distant. 'Oh, she's not well at all.'

'Really? Do tell me what's wrong. I've a very good doctor, you know.'

'It's nothing, really. She has trouble with her head. I think it's her head.'

'Migraine,' said Mrs Stevanson firmly, leading Heywood now into the drawing-room. 'I've been a martyr to it myself. You know,' and she lowered her voice, 'I think it's due to the change of life.'

'Really, Helena!' Heywood was gently shocked. He made a restraining motion with his white limp hairless hand. 'I'm sure she's much too young for that.'

'Well, you never can tell,' said Mrs Stevanson who knew Mrs Heywood's exact age.

'What a lot of people,' sighed Heywood. 'So many people.'

'There *are* a lot,' said Mrs Stevanson proudly. 'As usual I don't know half of them.'

Carefully she cut Mr Heywood away from her, allowed him to float unprotected through the groups of people. He looked back at her sadly but she had no pity for him and, finally, a group of Wall Street people swallowed him up and she saw him no more.

Several people were entering the drawing-room. They walked slowly with the carefully controlled uneasiness of people who didn't know the hostess well.

She recognized one of the newcomers and she greeted him joyfully : Ulysses returned to Ithaca, as the small Greek named Timon might have said.

The man she knew introduced her to the others. Most of them were English and she had a great admiration for the English. It was not particularly fashionable to like them now but she still was fascinated by them because they could talk without moving their lips. It *was* rather wonderful.

'And this,' said the man she knew, 'is Mrs Bankton.'

'How do you do,' said Mrs Bankton in a low voice. She was not English; Mrs Stevanson could tell that right away.

'We've met before, I think?' A hint of question was in Mrs Stevanson's voice.

'I don't think we have.'

Mrs Bankton was definitely not English. Her accent was French or Spanish or Italian. Mrs Stevanson could never tell one from the other.

'Mrs Bankton's husband is the artist,' said the man she knew slightly.

'Of course,' said Mrs Bankton wondering who Bankton was. 'Certainly, I know. But you're not English, my dear?'

'No, madam, I'm not English.' Mrs Bankton smiled at her and made no further admissions. Mrs Stevanson looked at her with dislike. She liked to find out about people quickly. Life was too short to have them hold back important facts and, ultimately, confidences. People always confided in Mrs Stevanson, knowing that she was not sufficiently interested in them to repeat what she heard.

'I do hope you'll enjoy yourself,' said Mrs Stevanson more cordially than she would have done had she liked the person.

'Thank you,' murmured Mrs Bankton. They bowed slightly to each other and parted. Mrs Stevanson watched Mrs Bankton as she walked across the room with her party. She looked very exotic in a short black lace dress and a red rose in her hair. What slim ankles, thought Mrs Stevanson disagreeably, thinking of her own heavy legs, practical legs one artist had told her, voluptuous legs an even better artist had said.

Mrs Stevanson turned, setting a smile on her lips. She faced the largest of all the groups : over twenty people talking all at once to each other. Holding her breasts high she approached them and, as she was recognized, their voices lowered and smiles appeared all about her and she was accepted into the centre of the group and there devoured.

Robert Holton was received by a butler. His coat was taken with ceremony and he was moved easily out of the black marble foyer into the drawing-room.

He had never visited Mrs Stevanson in her New York apartment. He was greatly impressed and he tried to retain a mental image of what he saw : he was constructing a dream world and such an apartment might be material for it.

The drawing-room was large, formal and very light. Three chandeliers hung from the high ceiling. The walls were panelled in white wood with gold-leaf decorations, like the palace at Versailles. Paintings hung at regular intervals about the room : portraits mostly, portraits of Mrs Stevanson. There was one large painting of a countryside which Robert Holton could tell immediately was done by Rembrandt or someone like him.

The room was thickly carpeted and tables and formal chairs furnished the room. A few people sat; most of them, however, preferred to stand, to move about gracefully, searching.

He stood blinking in the light, drugged by the high noise of voices, hypnotized by the odour of many flowers drenched over the women who stood talking to men.

He walked slowly, uncertain towards the centre of the room. He knew no one in the room. He looked for familiar faces, though; there were none. Then he saw Mrs Stevanson and he walked towards her. She looked at him and he could tell she was puzzled. Then she recognized him; she came towards him and they met beneath a portrait of her holding lilies.

'You're little Bob Holton, aren't you?' A strange description, he thought.

'Yes, Mrs Stevanson, you remember we met last year and...'

'Of course we did. How *is* your father?'

'Fine, just fine.' His father hated her.

'I'm so glad to hear that. I think you look more like your mother, you know. She was such a lovely woman.'

He mumbled thank you.

'Your mother was one of the most charming women I ever knew. She had such a wonderful way of doing things, so original.' Like marrying my father, thought Holton. 'She was always full of surprises. I used to enjoy her so much.'

There was an awkward silence. Robert Holton never found it easy to talk about his mother and Mrs Stevanson had decided, obviously, that it was the only thing she could discuss with him.

'It was very nice of you...' began Holton.

'Think nothing of it, my dear. I don't know if there are

98

many younger people here. You might look round, though. I suppose you'll know everybody. There's Laura Whitner over there . . . You know her of course.' He looked and saw a dark little woman wearing a skull cap.

'I've seen her act,' he said accurately.

'Oh, yes.' Mrs Stevanson looked around the room. He could see that she was preparing to leave him alone.

He was wrong. 'You must,' she said, 'meet some friends of mine. They're foreigners and they've only just arrived. They don't know anyone . . .' She was going to say 'either' but did not.

She led him over to a small group of men and women. Mrs Stevanson didn't know their names but she acted as if they were her dearest friends.

'This young man is Robert Holton. His mother was a great friend of mine and you must be nice to him.' She was cute. 'He's just got out of the navy.' She looked up suddenly with a magnificent gesture, looked as if someone had hailed her from across the room. 'Oh I have to go! Please excuse me.' She moved away in a swirl of silk, her bright blue hair bouncing on the back of her thick white neck.

'How do you do,' said Holton, shaking hands with a dark man. Then he shook hands with a light man, with a short heavy one, with a thin blonde girl and finally he shook hands with Mrs Bankton.

'How do you do,' said Robert Holton.

'How do *you* do,' said Mrs Bankton. Her voice startled him. It was deep and foreign and she had said the 'you' as though she had really meant him.

'I'm very well,' he said and he looked at her. Her hair was dark. Her eyes were greenish and bright and shining. He looked at her mouth, red and curved, elfinly shaped. He stammered, 'I know you. I know you but . . .'

'But who am I?' She laughed and gestured with her long white hands.

'Yes, who are you?'

'Carla.'

'No!'

'Yes.'

'You've changed. I . . .'

'And so have you. I think you look younger out of uniform.'

'But . . .'

'You're surprised to see me? I'm just visiting this country. My husband,' she paused, 'my husband is in England and I think he'll be coming to join me soon.'

'Then you're married?'

'But of course! And very well.' She smiled at him, smiled gently and he felt embarrassed because she acknowledged an old relationship so easily; that she was so unmoved, so unguilty.

'I'm very happy to hear that.' He didn't know what else to say.

'Thank you. Let's get out of this crowd.' She looked about her. She pointed to a corner of the room, an alcove containing a window. 'Let's go over there.' They walked through the crowd and sat down on the love seat beneath the window.

'You're surprised, aren't you?' She spoke softly.

'A little, I guess. I don't know. I have to get used to the idea. I always associated you with . . . with Florence and . . .'

'You felt that was behind you?'

He was surprised. She must have known him very well, he thought suddenly; he had forgotten how well she had known him. 'No, I didn't think that,' he lied.

'I have very warm memories,' she said lightly.

He blushed and hated himself but there was nothing he could do or say that would make it better. 'Mine were pleasant, too. I . . . I liked Florence quite a bit.'

'Yes, I'm sure you did, and you liked Fiesole, and the nights and summer days. I suppose you liked them all.'

'I liked them all.'

'And that was what you liked, all that you can remember?'

'No, I *remember* more. I . . . I didn't know if you'd want to talk about that; being married and . . .'

She was surprised. 'But I knew you first, after all. That counts for something and then I remembered, too. It hasn't been so long.'

'Several years.'

'It doesn't seem that long to me. You remember those nights at our place in Fiesole? We used to go out and sit on the ledge and look at the lights of the city.' They both looked out of the window then, looked at the glacier-bright squares of light.

'It was very pretty.'

'You Anglo-Saxon!' She laughed at him, not maliciously but gaily. 'You say it's pretty. You say it's nice. It was beautiful and you know it. That was a beautiful time.'

He felt her warmth suddenly, began to remember her warmth, began to remember much that he had forgotten. 'Yes,' said he, warmed by her, 'those *nights* were beautiful.'

'Good, I wanted to hear you say that. I wanted you to say,' her voice became so low that he could barely hear her, 'I wanted you to say much more but I think you've forgotten.' She looked out at the towers of the city, at the glittering webs of light. She was embarrassed now and he was not. No, she was not embarrassed; he realized that with a sudden vision; she was sad and he didn't want her to be sad.

'You know . . . I can say more. I didn't think you wanted to hear it. That was so long ago. You're married and . . .'

She turned around and faced him, her face alive and gay; her moods changed so quickly, he remembered: he had always been baffled by her changes. 'You got interested in someone else. I know what you soldiers are like. Italians are just the same in Italy.'

'No, there isn't anyone else.' This was the wrong thing to say and he tried to withdraw the words from the air but they were lost to him now.

'No one else? No one . . .?'

'Well . . .'

'How strange.' She looked at a painting of Mrs Stevanson and at that moment she looked as if this painting were the most important thing to her. Finally she said, 'I think I'd like to drink some whisky. Shall we go to the bar?'

'Certainly, Carla.' He was glad that he had said her name naturally.

Carla felt uncertain. The cold glass that a footman had given her was chilling her hand. She wondered if she should put it down on the dining-room table. They were standing near it and Robert Holton was looking hungrily at the food; she could see that in a moment he would have enough courage to eat.

'What a dreadful room,' said Carla.

'What?' He looked at her as though she had not been there. 'Oh, yes, it's sort of forbidding.' He glanced at the dark wood-pannelled walls and the ornate chandelier.

'I don't know why these people must have everything so heavy inside,' said Carla. 'The buildings in New York are so tall and light.'

'Some places are more modern.'

'I suppose they are.' The glass of whisky in her hand was becoming much too cold to hold. She put it down on the table.

'You don't like it?'

'I think I've had enough for now. You remember how little I used to drink.'

'Yes, you never needed it.' He looked at her directly and smiled. She was happy then because it was the first time he had looked at her eyes. He was losing his fear of her, this strange and, to her, inexplicable fear.

'Let's find some place to sit down,' she said.

'I thought you wanted to walk around.'

She laughed. 'All right, we'll do both.' They walked around.

More people had arrived. Several hundred, thought Carla with distaste. She liked smaller parties. She had only come tonight because friends of her husband had insisted. They were keeping close watch over her for they knew how jealous Bankton was. It was very amusing, she thought as she and Holton walked from group to group. Her husband's friends watching her now would never suspect what had happened in Florence.

They came to an especially large group, a dozen men surrounding Laura Whitner.

'Do you want to meet her?' asked Carla, looking at Holton, knowing that he did.

'You don't know her?'

'But of course. I know everyone.'

They cut their way through the bewitched men, cut through to the enchantress herself.

Laura Whitner was dark and slight with full breasts. Her face was as delicate as a carving in ivory; sallow, too, as old ivory. The lips were brilliant red and she twisted her mouth in childlike expressions and her sad dark eyes glittered from habit and not from fire. She looked unwell, thought Carla.

'Carla Bruno!' exclaimed Laura when she saw them. The two women embraced with warmth and the enchantment was broken for the admirers and they began to withdraw from the circle of her spell, smiling as they departed, leaving her alone in her theatre with only two admirers.

'But my tiny Carla, what are you doing in New York? I haven't seen you for years, not since Paris.'

'I'm here visiting.'

'But I'm so happy to see you! You know, you're the last person I'd expect to run into here.'

'I had to get away from Europe. I hadn't been to America since I was a child.'

Laura Whitner looked at her hands. 'You're not married, are you?' Carla wore no wedding ring.

Carla smiled and nodded.

Laura looked astonished, her scarlet mouth, like a wicked child's, twisted with all the emotions she felt and several that she did not. 'To whom? To the little one here?' She motioned to Robert Holton who had been standing silently watching her.

Carla laughed. 'No, Laura, to Bankton in England.'

'The painter?'

'The painter. We've been married two years.'

'Are you happy?' There was a dark note in her voice as she said this and Carla could tell that it was something she wanted to know.

'I am not unhappy,' said Carla, knowing that this was no answer but she hoped that Holton would grasp her meaning.

103

'I'm sorry,' said Laura Whitner almost undramatically. 'I married again, you know.'

'I heard you did. Is he here tonight? I used to know him.'

'He couldn't come, he's working on a show. Are you going to have children?'

'I don't think so.'

'I want one.' She sighed and touched the skullcap on her head with a hand that was pale and like the claw of a bird, a hand that shook. 'If I'm not too old I'm going to make a child. I think that's what I need.'

'You must be very happy with him.'

She nodded and said with great sincerity, 'Yes, I'm very happy now. After a long time I am.' And Carla looked into her sad dark eyes and saw that they had not changed expression.

'Who is this?' asked Laura Whitner, turning to Holton, making love to him automatically with her face.

'This,' said Carla, 'is Robert Holton, an old friend of mine. We knew each other in Florence during the war.'

'Indeed!' She lifted her thin brows and made her mouth very round. Holton blushed and Carla wanted to protect him.

'I'm very pleased to meet you,' said Holton awkwardly. 'I've liked you in the movies.' Carla remembered then his honesty : the thing that had attracted her to him. He had always been honest; she wondered if that was so now.

'Have you really, child? Thank you.' She made a gesture that was intended for an entire audience but it was still very graceful.

'You must,' said Carla, 'call me up and we'll get together. I'm staying at the Mason.'

'I shall, of course. Tell me . . .' At this moment Mrs Raymond Stevanson appeared to capture Laura.

'Laura, darling, I've got the most marvellous Estonian who wants to meet you. I think he said he was an Estonian. I know you'll love him. You'll excuse me, I know.' She said this last to Carla and Holton.

'We'll have lunch,' said Laura, calling back over her shoulder as she was borne away by the conquering Mrs Stevanson.

'What did you think of her, Bob?' asked Carla.

'She's not as pretty as I thought she'd be.'

'They never are; you must learn that.'

He looked at her and she tried to tell what he was thinking but for once her intuition was not enough : she had first to examine the years that had gone by. She had to find some trace of familiar emotion in him. She had to rediscover the stranger. She had to make him remember what she remembered. In Florence he had loved her, she was sure of that. Now it was up to her to reconstruct a passion that had never been wholly lost. She had cared more for him than he had known then; would ever know, she hoped. There had been so many nights after he had left when she had longed to be with him, nights when she could feel again the warm summer about them as they lay together in the wide bed in her room. She was determined now to find the lover in the stranger that stood beside her, who stood looking seriously but remotely into her face.

'Shall we sit down now, Bob?'

People were beginning to leave. It was eight-thirty and Mrs Stevanson was glad to see them go. The first two hours were interesting and then she found herself bored.

On the other hand George *Robert* Lewis was not bored. He was slightly drunk and enjoying himself very much. He was usually overcome by a monstrous *ennui* during the day which, as evening came, grew less and less. In a few more hours he would have discovered a reason for living and this would keep him happy until he woke up the next morning with a hang-over.

He was glad when he heard that the famous Bankton's wife was at the party. She had been pointed out to him but he hadn't met her yet. He stopped a waiter and took a cocktail from him. And, equipped for conversation with a woman, he marched across the drawing-room to where Carla stood talking with a young man, a rather nice young man, thought Lewis.

'Mrs Bankton?'

She turned and looked at him and he rather liked her brown-green eyes.

'Yes?' She looked at him as though she wanted him to go away. Lewis was sensitive to such things but not particularly nonplussed; in fact he was accustomed to being asked to go away.

'I'm George *Robert* Lewis . . . you know *Regarde*, the *avant garde* magazine, only it's so trite now to call anything *avant garde*. You must have seen it. We did the most splendid article on Bankton last year. I've just loved his work because I can feel what he's trying to do : post-surrealism and all that sort of thing. I'm all for it; in fact, we're all for people like Bankton who do things. I just felt I couldn't help but come over and say hello.'

She smiled at him very nicely. 'I've heard of you, Mr Lewis. My husband thinks very highly of what your magazine is doing.'

'He does? Oh, but isn't that simply marvellous! I always felt I would be most sympathetic with the great Bankton. Tell me, darling, when do you expect him in this country?'

She took the 'darling' quite well, Holton thought.

'I'm not sure. I think in a month or so. He's so busy in London. By the way,' she said, 'I want you to meet an old friend of mine, Robert Holton.'

'Very pleased to meet you, Mr Lewis,' said the young man as they shook hands.

'*Enchanté*,' said Lewis, bowing from the waist and allowing his hand to stay too long in Holton's. Such a nice young man, thought Lewis, and wondered if . . .

'What,' said Carla, 'is *Regarde* espousing now?' She spoke quickly and Lewis could see that she understood him and this pleased him although, in a sense, they were rivals.

'As always, the advanced, the revolutionary . . .'

'And the honest?'

'But of course, darling, we are never consciously dishonest, though it *is* hard sometimes not being.'

'Perhaps in life but not in art.' She spoke severely. She was a Latin; he could tell now from her accent.

'You're not English?' He changed the subject.

'No, I'm a Florentine.'

106

'But how charming! I have always loved Florence. I spent several summers there when I was a boy. Let me see . . . I was there last in 19 . . . It's not important. How I loved those doors, though!'

He saw that the young man named Robert Holton was beginning to look bored and Lewis hated above all else to be thought a bore even by a bore.

'And *you* have been to Florence?'

Holton nodded.

Carla said, 'That was where we met the first time. He's an old friend of our family's.'

'How droll that must've been for you, finding this charming boy here at Helena Stevanson's who, though I love her dearly, gives the dullest parties in New York.'

'They *are* dull. I wonder why people come. Why do you come?'

'I'm a creature in constant need of companionship. I go to everything. I *must* see a lot of people or I become most dreadfully morbid and then I write poems.'

She smiled. 'I remember you used to write some good poems.'

He laughed, pleased. 'You remember then? That was so long ago. I somehow have got all out of the habit.'

'Perhaps you see too many people.'

'That may be right and, speaking of people, you lovely ones must have dinner with me this evening, otherwise I must eat alone; I've been deserted today by everyone.'

'I'm afraid,' said Carla, 'that we can't . . .'

'That's not a bad idea,' said Holton much to Lewis's surprise – to Carla's surprise, too. Lewis looked at her and saw she was surprised. He was amused, wickedly amused. There was something between them.

'You must really join me. I know of the most interesting place in the Village. I know you'll love it.'

'Don't you want to go?' asked Holton, looking at Carla.

'Why . . .' She didn't know what to say.

'Certainly you'll come; three is good company.'

Carla gestured uncertainly with her hands.

'Perhaps I'd better come back in a moment,' said Lewis,

smiling maliciously at Carla. 'I so hope I'm not upsetting plans.' He made bowing movements and retreated into the centre of the party.

As he withdrew he could see the long look Carla gave the young man.

The men from Wall Street bored Mr Heywood. He tried to act like them but from time to time he could not help implying gently to them that he was a broker through heredity, not inclination. It was so much easier doing what his father had done than to do anything else or nothing at all. He had a puritanical horror of doing nothing. His family had made him believe that it was necessary always to work and he rather liked the work, too. It made him think less about his own uniquely miserable life.

His wives were a large part of the general dreariness of his life. He never seemed to marry the right women. They either wanted his money or wanted to dominate him. He was used to domination by now but it made him uneasy sometimes to feel that his own will was so easily bent by others. He was always making stands, erecting firm barriers, but somehow the barriers usually collapsed. He wondered sometimes if he shouldn't collect stamps or have a hobby like that.

Thinking of this, he began now to divorce himself from the group of Wall Street people. He promised to have lunch with one, to call up another; he bowed to a third, shook hands with a fourth and then he floated softly away, a look of quiet happiness on his face : he was now alone in the midst of a party.

Mr Heywood looked about him to see if there was anyone he might like to talk to. He would prefer some young woman who looked lonely. His three wives had all looked lonely at one period of the courtship and he had married them as much for this corresponding loneliness as for anything else. He had been mistaken three times but he was, in general, an optimist.

There seemed to be no lonely-looking young woman. He sighed and was about to leave the party when he saw Robert

Holton. He remembered him clearly; he was proud of his memory. Now he would have to speak to him. It would be difficult, but then he had always been taught that if a thing was particularly unpleasant it should be done : character was made in this fashion and character was more important than anything else. He proceeded to mould his character. He walked towards Robert Holton.

Mr Heywood approached Holton from behind and he could overhear his conversation with a dark pretty woman.

Holton was saying, 'I think it might be interesting. After all, Carla, I don't get out much and if a person like Lewis wants us to go I think we should.'

'If you want to, Bob.' She was a foreigner, thought Mr Heywood with interest. 'I'd hoped we might have had dinner together and try to . . . to talk of . . . I'm not saying this well, I'm sorry.'

'No, Carla . . .' Mr Heywood drifted between them now. 'Mr Holton?' he asked.

'Oh, Mr Heywood! How do you do, sir?' Robert Holton was impressed as always with Mr Heywood's greatness and this both saddened and pleased Mr Heywood.

'I had thought . . .' began Mr Heywood in a barely audible voice.

'This,' said Holton quickly on top of Mr Heywood's words, 'is Mrs Bankton, an old friend of mine. Mr Heywood.'

The meeting was made and Mr Heywood was rather attracted to this pretty girl who spoke English so beautifully and yet with an accent.

'I thought I should find you here, Mr Holton. Mrs Stevanson was telling me about you.'

'That was nice of her.'

'She is a charming woman,' said Mr Heywood, praising an absent person about whom they all cared very little; it filled the first awkwardness of a meeting such as this. 'You enjoy being downtown?' He was careful not to associate himself with Holton's job.

'Oh, very much,' said Holton.

'By the way,' asked the dark pretty woman, 'what are you doing now? You haven't told me.'

109

Holton flushed and Mr Heywood was sorry for him. 'I'm working in a brokerage office.'

She laughed. 'But how dreadful that must be.'

Holton looked miserable and Mr Heywood, who rather agreed with her, laughed. 'It's not too terrible, Mrs Bankton. Some of us manage to survive it. I think a sense of humour is the most important thing.'

'I'm sorry,' she said. 'I had no idea you were also in the same situation.'

How delightful she was, thought Mr Heywood. 'We must all,' said Mr Heywood in a voice that was like the sigh of a dying man, 'do our appointed tasks. Duty is of such great importance: it is the only tangible thing in the chaos of living.'

'But I don't think that's so at all,' said Carla as gently as he but with less resignation. 'One should always try to do what one wants to do.'

'In spite of one's duty to others?'

'People that you love?'

'No, that I . . . that one admires and respects.'

'And this makes you happy?'

'Are any of us happy?' asked Heywood in a voice of weary sadness; he stopped, suddenly remembering that young Holton was there. It would never do for him to hear these things.

'I talked,' he said casually 'with Murphy about you today. He seemed most enthusiastic.'

'That's nice. I like working with him.'

'Perhaps,' said Mr Heywood, looking at a spot somewhere over Holton's head, 'perhaps you would be interested in working in the jobs that, ah, come in contact with the public.' He could not say selling: he tried but he could not. He wondered if maybe a long trip to South America would give him a new perspective.

'I think that would be wonderful!' Holton was moved as he should be. An affable young man, thought Mr Heywood who, as a rule, did not like men at all, especially young men who seemed to be able to get all the lonely young women they wanted.

'Perhaps,' murmured Mr Heywood, 'something can be

arranged in the near future.' He looked at the dark woman beside Holton and he thought her an unusually real person to find in such a place as this. She was probably not real, though : only an illusion with long white hands and silvery nails. He was used to women vanishing.

George *Robert* Lewis appeared and Mr Heywood experienced a slight spasm of nausea. He found Lewis hard to be with. Mr Heywood would not have said that being a broker was a productive life but if, to be an artist, it was necessary to be like Lewis he had no desire to be an artist.

'How do you do?' said Lewis, bowing very low and smirking at him.

'And how are you?' inquired Mr Heywood politely, beginning to retreat slowly.

'Doing marvellously. These charming people here are dining with me, aren't you?'

Carla looked uncertain and Holton nodded. Mr Heywood wondered where Holton had run across Lewis.

'I'm really,' said Lewis in a conspiratorial voice (an old woman's voice, thought Mr Heywood, frowning slightly), 'just doing a job. Her husband is one of our idols and I may get a perfectly marvellous essay out of her. I knew his work so well.' Mr Heywood wondered vaguely why Lewis was explaining so many things.

'I see,' said Mr Heywood. He turned to Carla. 'Delighted to have met you.' He nodded to Holton. 'I shall probably see you tomorrow.'

'Yes, sir; good night, sir.' Mr Heywood glided away towards the door.

Mrs Stevanson appeared beside him just as he had made up his mind to leave.

'Do cheer up, Heywood. You look so petulant !'

'I'm not really, Helena, not really.'

'I'm not sure. Who're you looking at?' He glanced away quickly but she saw that he had been watching Carla. 'Lovely, isn't she? I'm afraid she's stuck with that Holton boy and, my Lord, George *Robert*'s got her too. The poor child and . . .' Mrs Stevanson was surprised. 'I do think they're leaving !'

'After all,' said Heywood soothingly, 'it *is* a cocktail party. They probably weren't able to find you.'

'I suppose you're right, Heywood. Manners change so. She looked rather unhappy, I thought.'

'Who?'

'Mrs Bankton.'

'Really. I didn't notice.'

'I don't suppose you did; men don't notice very many things anyway,' said Mrs Stevanson, suddenly exhibiting her bitterness. She controlled herself quickly. 'Except men like you, Heywood dear.'

'Thank you, Helena.' He bowed without movement; he suggested a bow without actually executing it. 'Now I must really be going.'

'So soon, Heywood, so soon?'

TEN

Carla was angry with Robert Holton, angrier still with George *Robert* Lewis. She had hoped to have dinner alone with Holton. She wanted time to recover a past emotion and now she would have very little time. As they drove through the lighted streets she looked with dislike at Lewis's smooth boyish face.

None of them spoke after they got into the cab outside Mrs Stevanson's place. Lewis had given the driver an address and they had relaxed, each thinking of different things: Holton pleased to be seeing life; Lewis pleased to have secured the wife of a great figure; Carla displeased with the arrangement, Carla plotting murder.

Robert Holton sat in the middle. Carla had decided that if she had to spend an evening with Lewis she at least wouldn't sit next to him.

She looked at Holton as they drove down Seventh Avenue. He was looking straight ahead. His well-formed, not very strong mouth was set in a straight line; he was trying to be firm now; he was trying to convince her that he was right in accepting Lewis's invitation for them.

She sighed loudly so that she would be heard and understood. Then she looked out the window and examined the neon signs that broke the darkness with many colours. She liked the lights.

The taxicab stopped on a side street where a dozen or more signs advertised night clubs. They got out and Lewis paid the driver.

'Where is it?' asked Holton, looking about him.

Lewis pointed to some steps, 'Right down there. I suppose

it's open; you know, there was some talk that the police might close it but I don't think they will. Shall we go in?'

Carla could see that Holton was wondering what he meant when he said that the police might close it. She understood herself and she was rather pleased now : it would be a lesson for him, an experience that he needed.

Lewis led them down the steps and into the night club.

There were two large rooms : one light and garish, with a long bar, many mirrors and boots; the other was darker, with tables and, at one end, a small band on a small stage. They went into the darker room. The headwaiter recognized Lewis and was very polite to him; he showed them to a table near the stage.

'Isn't this charming?' asked Lewis. 'I think it has a wonderful atmosphere.' He grinned at Carla. She nodded.

'It's not too garish,' she said. 'So many American places are too light.'

'Do they have a floor show?' asked Holton.

'A very unusual one,' said Lewis, giggling. 'I'm sure you'll think it great fun. Hermes de Bianca is the star of the show and his dance is perfectly magnificent. He is one of the great artists, great interpretive artists, I mean.'

'Is that right?'

A waiter came to take their order. He was a curious-looking waiter, a type which Carla recognized but Holton did not. He wore no uniform. She looked around the room and found that none of the others wore uniforms. They were dressed casually. This waiter's hair was long, unpleasantly long and the front of it had been carefully bleached. He was thin and moved stiffly, self-consciously, like a woman thinking of rape. On one of his fingers he wore a large ring with a bizarre stone in it.

'What do you people want?' His voice was irritable and high. He was looking interestedly at Holton who was looking just as interestingly at him.

'I'd love something to drink,' said Lewis. 'How about the rest of you?'

The waiter looked at Lewis for the first time. His face

brightened. 'George, it's you! How lovely to see you! You haven't been here in such a long time.'

'I've been dreadfully busy,' said Lewis coldly, disengaging himself from the waiter's assumed relationship.

'I think,' said Holton, 'that I'd like a highball.' They all decided to have the same thing and the waiter, with a slight toss of his head, walked away.

The small band was playing loudly and eagerly. One sentimental modern song after another was catapulted into the room. Fortunately, after several minutes the band stopped playing and the musicians departed.

'I'm glad they're gone,' said Carla. 'They make too much music.'

'They aren't very delicate.' Lewis turned suddenly to Holton. 'And you, what do you do?'

Holton flushed. 'Well, I work in a brokerage house.'

Lewis's eyebrows went up and he elaborately showed surprise and disbelief. 'But how remarkable! You're not an artist! Surely you must do something wonderful. You have the hands of an artist. You're just working there because you have to. That's it, isn't it?'

'No, that's not it.' Carla admired his courage. 'I don't mind working there and it's probably going to be my career.' His jaw got very firm. She liked him this way.

'How marvellous!' exclaimed Lewis. 'A contented Babbitt.' He stopped. 'What a dreadful thing to say : that's such a Nineteen-Twenty phrase. Really, I sometimes wonder if art *is* the answer to our problems.'

'I think it might be the artist,' said Carla softly.

Lewis bowed. '*Touché*, my dear. Let's say the dedication to art, the freedom from conventions. Perhaps this young man's view is the saner : to accept the pattern.' He was mocking now but he did not show it in his face.

'Some things you have to accept,' said Holton, aware of Lewis's mockery. 'Sometimes there is nothing else.'

'There is always something else,' said Lewis decidedly.

'I think that's right,' said Carla.

'What?' asked Holton. 'What else can you do but that?'

'Run away,' said Lewis.

'Fall in love,' said Carla.

But neither solution was convincing to Holton and Carla could think of no way to explain herself. There seemed, at the moment, no words to record her meaning, no bridge to reach him. They were all three quiet, thinking of questions and answers.

Finally their silence killed the problem and they began to notice the room they were in and the other people. The people at the different tables were not, generally, mixed. Several women would sit at one table and several men would sit at another. Around the room were small tables for two and here men sat with men and women with women. This was puzzling to Holton, she could see. He said nothing, though, and she had a great sudden ache of tenderness for him, a desire to protect his innocence. But this she could not do. She was a stranger to him and he had forgotten.

Cigarette smoke veiled the room bluely and everything seemed tenuous and unreal. The sound of voices and ice clattering, of forks striking plates and of many people moving and breathing together made an ocean-like roar in Carla's ears. The room was hot and the smell of perfume was strong.

The band returned and began to play. They played much more softly than they had before and she was grateful. Conversation was not difficult when the music was soft. In fact, the music seemed to underline many things, made emotional statements dramatic. Unfortunately, with George *Robert* Lewis sitting at the table there was no opportunity to make emotional statements. He would have to leave. She began to concentrate on this as they talked now of trivial things. Finally he received her subconscious message. He stood up.

'I hope you'll excuse me a moment but I have to go backstage. I'll only be gone a minute.' He left quickly, going around the stage and behind the crimson curtain.

'He's a funny little queer, isn't he?' commented Holton.

'He's one of the great aesthetes. You're glad you came tonight?'

'It's interesting,' he said. He was defending himself now.

'This is a very . . .' she paused, trying to think of the right word, 'trivial world. I don't think you'll like it.'

'Perhaps I will. I used to be something of a sculptor.' He said this laughing, and she could see that he was quite serious.

'Then why don't you do it?'

'I wasn't good enough. I haven't done any since I was in college.

'Would you like to do it?'

'I don't think so.' She couldn't tell whether he meant this or not.

The waiter came and put their glasses down on the table with a look of boredom; in fact, he yawned slightly as he did it. He tried to catch Holton's eye but failed. Sulkily he walked away.

'I don't want this,' said Carla, pointing to the glass.

'I'll take it,' said Holton and he began to drink his own, his teeth making clicking sounds as the ice bobbed against them.

'You like what you're doing now?' asked Carla.

He put the glass down and frowned. 'I suppose I do. I have to do it and so I figure I might as well like it.'

'Perhaps you might find something you like better.'

'What?'

'You might be a sculptor again.'

He laughed. 'I'm really no good. I can't do anything else but this, I don't see anything wrong with what I'm doing, anyway.'

'There's nothing wrong with it if you're happy; are you?'

He didn't answer for a moment. Then he said, 'I suppose I am.'

'But you're not in love?'

'What has that to do with it?'

'So many things,' said Carla and she did not look at him; she avoided his eyes. He did not understand. She could see that now. The desire, however, to make him destroy his barriers, to come alive, was becoming an obsession with her. And then, of course, he had been the first man she had known and that made him important to her. She had never lost her feeling for him and she was sad to see him confused; Carla thought of herself as Joan of Arc: helping the king to

117

his throne. She was not yet sure, however, that the king wished to reign.

The music was becoming soft and sentimental. Full round chords gushed around them and people danced on the stage. Men danced with women and women with men for there was not really much courage among these people.

'Would you like to dance?' asked Holton.

'Not right now.'

He was not disappointed. She watched him as he watched the other people in the room. This was something new for him. She guessed that he was shocked by the people he saw at the different tables. He showed nothing in his face, though. Perhaps he did not recognize them, did not know them the way she did : she who had married one of them.

'It's been quite a while, hasn't it?' said Holton finally.

'Yes, but I haven't forgotten any of it, have you?'

'Of course not. Naturally I didn't know whether you wanted to talk about it. I figured that . . . well, after you married Bankton you wouldn't want to think about what we did.'

'I don't,' said Carla, 'love Bankton.'

He was shocked and she knew that she had said the right thing if in the wrong manner.

'But you got married,' said Holton.

She nodded. 'I'm afraid I didn't know very much about him then. I went to London after the war was over and I stayed with some artists there. I met him and he made love to me. I thought he was very wonderful. I had heard stories about him : that he was . . . was like these people here.' She gestured to include the room. 'I didn't believe the stories. I married him. I found he wanted me for camouflage.'

'Why don't you divorce him then?'

'Perhaps I shall someday. It seems so much trouble, though. He's really a very nice person.'

Holton shook his head, confused. 'I don't see . . . I don't see why he married you in the first place if he was . . .'

'He could still like me, Bob.'

'I don't see how.'

She smiled. 'It *is* hard to explain but anyway you know

118

now that I don't feel too deeply about him. You understand this?'

'I suppose so,' said Robert Holton. He *is* beginning to understand, thought Carla, happy now : her words had begun to build the bridge between them. Soon they would meet again.

'You've certainly had a funny life,' said Holton smiling.

'Sometimes I think so but then the most important thing is making a freedom for oneself. When that's done nothing is strange because everything is natural. You know what I mean?'

He nodded. 'Sometimes I know.'

She picked up a fork and drew pictures on the white tablecloth. 'I want you to be free,' she said.

'Free from what?'

'You know. From your routine and morals : the things you don't want.'

He laughed. 'You know pretty well what my set of morals is and I don't mind the routine so much.'

'I think you do.'

'Why?'

'Why did you want to come here with Lewis tonight? Why are you with me now?'

He smiled. 'Perhaps you're partly right. I was curious and I do get bored and ...'

'And you're alone.' She spoke for him.

He finished his drink and did not answer her; there was no need to answer her.

'Are you glad,' she asked at last, 'are you glad to see me again?'

He said that he was. He declared that he was. He made an issue of it. He was still not at ease with her and she felt desperate. It was like a battle between them; first one side retreating and the other advancing ... Or perhaps a hunt. She was the hunter and her memories the pursued. She knew that beneath his many assumed faces there was the person she had known in Florence. Deliberately Carla began to smash the faces.

George *Robert* Lewis had a very pleasant interview with

de Bianca, the star; after a half-hour, though, he was beginning to get restless. Dancers seldom talked about anything interesting. Finally he excused himself, saying that his guests were waiting for him.

They were talking quietly and intimately when he got back to the table. He took a secret pleasure in interrupting them. Lewis had already decided they were lovers.

'I'm so dreadfully sorry that I went off and left you the way I did. It was stupid of me but I got so involved with Hermes and his amours : he tells me all about them and though they're really quite dull I have to be polite and listen. Have you ordered yet?'

They said that they had not. Lewis immediately became noisily efficient. He ordered the languid waiter about, gave him careful instructions and ignored his glances and meaningful gestures. Lewis never had liked this type at all. The ones like this waiter never seemed to have any respect for him. They couldn't understand the principles for which he stood. They were not artists.

The dinner finally ordered, he turned towards his guests, a white-toothed smile on his slightly rouged lips (Hermes had lent him rouge).

'Are you adoring the atmosphere, my dear Mrs Bankton? It's nothing to compare with Paris, of course, but you must admit that it's a lot gayer than Rome. I love Rome and usually have a marvellous time there but somehow one never seems to find the same easy atmosphere that we have here.'

'No, it is not like Rome,' agreed Carla. What wonderful golden skin she has, thought Lewis, enjoying her aesthetically. He didn't dislike women the way many of his friends did. He felt, in fact, most compatible with them.

'Are there many places like this in New York?' asked Holton. Lewis was pleased that he had caught on. Lewis, always optimistic, wondered if it might not be possible to make some sort of an arrangement . . . It was not impossible, certainly.

'Oh, quite a few, quite a few. They *are* rather charming from time to time. I enjoy visiting them and I do feel that the atmosphere is not uncongenial.' He wondered if perhaps he hadn't been using the word 'atmosphere' too much.

'I've heard about these places,' said Holton without much expression.

'Surely you don't disapprove?' Lewis was intent on discovering this now. He could see that Carla was uneasy. Holton was unsatisfactory, though.

'I don't care much one way or the other,' he said and he turned to Carla and began to talk to her again. Lewis, disappointed, listened to them as they talked of Fiesole.

Lewis was not quite sure what their relationship was. As they talked he gathered that she was more interested than he in continuing it. That was usually the case, however. Young men like Holton were apt to be a little unfeeling, a little stuffy. George *Robert* Lewis thought pleasantly of young men.

When he felt that they had talked too long without him, he interrupted. 'When were you last in Fiesole?' He looked at Carla, intending the question for her; it was difficult not having a name to call her.

She looked at him as though she had forgotten him completely. 'In Fiesole? I was there just a year ago.'

'I suppose it's pretty well recovered from the war. I told you how I used to love visiting there before the war. I hope it will always be pleasant.'

'I think it will,' said Carla.

'Europe must've been very nice before the war,' said Holton.

George *Robert* Lewis made an elaborate motion to show just what it had been before the war; as he was finishing his movement the waiter brought them their dinner: a number of dishes with filet of sole at the centre.

'I hope you enjoy it,' said the waiter spitefully, putting the dishes down loudly and angrily. He walked away, his duty done.

Lewis sighed. 'These dreadful waiters, they presume so. I suppose that it's part of the American dream. Shall we begin?' Like a priest of a pagan cult he began to perform the ritual of arranging plates, of removing covers, of neatly moving food from plate to plate, and finally of eating. The others imitated him.

'When,' asked Robert Holton, after the main part of the dinner had been eaten, 'will the show start?'

Lewis put down his fork carefully, swallowed, and said, 'Very soon, I think. What time is it?' There was an examining of watches: ten-fifteen. 'The show starts at ten-thirty. I hope you're not impatient. The audience is very often as interesting as the show. But I must say that de Bianca's dance is in another world and that we mustn't miss it. I'll be very curious to know how you react.'

'There used to be a place in Paris like this where they had a wonderful dancer of the same type. I suppose he's the type of dancer I think he is?' said Carla.

'He is quite probably the sort of dancer you think he is,' said Lewis, smiling, excluding Holton from his words. 'The only difference is that he is a great artist, interpretive artist, I mean. I know you'll appreciate him.'

A group of people who knew Lewis came over to their table. They acted most respectfully and he hoped that Carla and Holton were noticing what an important person he was. He spoke nicely to them, shook hands with them, and let them know that he was busy. They left him then, smiling. Smiling himself, he turned to Carla and Holton and he was disappointed to find them talking together again. Holton had taken Carla's hand in his and Lewis felt a strange anguish, felt an inward betrayal. He did not know what had been betrayed, however.

'I'm sorry, my dear, that I didn't introduce you to those people. It was rude of me because they *all* admire your husband's work.'

'That's perfectly all right,' said Carla. 'I know so little about his work. I'm only a layman, you know.'

'I can hardly believe that. You must've been an artist yourself at one time.'

She shook her head. 'No, I was never an artist at anything. Except at living, perhaps.' Trumpets sounded loudly from the band, giving her statement an absurd grandeur. She sensed this and laughed. 'I wish to say that I try to make life a complete thing.'

'But what a marvellous thing to want to do! All of us try

that but when we fail at it (and alas we most of us fail) then we must find ourselves a medium to guard our egos, to protect our fears.'

'That's for the talented Mr Lewis but for the rest of us, the majority, only our lives count. We must make them natural.'

'And that,' said Robert Holton suddenly, 'is for the rich to do. The rest of us can't even do that.'

'How delightful!' exclaimed Lewis. 'We have here the three representatives of humanity : the rich and ... free? the poor and trapped, and the artist who is finding both freedom and an opiate. But how wonderfully symbolic! We're practically an allegory. I suppose we can reach some understanding.'

'How?' asked Holton and Lewis could see that he was asking Carla, not him. 'How can you get what you want without money? I don't see how you can ever do what you want if you aren't free.'

'I think,' said Carla, 'that you can become free. You can get free in art and you can get free in love. Money hasn't much to do with it. You can go anywhere alone. I don't think it's possible to be sane alone, without love.'

'I think you're right,' said Lewis sincerely and sadly, allowing the now soft music to dissolve his mind into an emotional waste out of which, of course, came art. 'I think you have explained all the tragedies in the world.'

'And all the happiness,' murmured Carla, looking at Holton. Holton smiled then. It was the first time that Lewis had seen him smile and he was struck by the gentleness and beauty of his face. He was beginning to see the person under the rather rigid mask and he understood now why this quiet wonderful woman was in love. Holton was about to say something when the band made a crescendo and the lights on the stage went up. The show was about to begin.

A slender little man, ineptly painted, appeared on the stage and welcomed the audience to the night club.

He then motioned and the lights in the room went out leaving only the stage with its curtain backdrop lighted. The

band began to play a current song and the master of cere-
monies proceeded to sing, using new dirty lyrics which made
the audience laugh. He then told a joke about fairies. The
audience laughed loudly at this revelling in exposure; often
their masks became too tight, too heavy. He removed them.

Finished with his joke, he bowed and several persons came
on to the stage. They were probably men. They wore dresses
and several of them had faces of great beauty. They danced,
parodying women, transcending the single sex. And in the
audience people looked at one another and nodded and
looked again at the stage, smiles on their faces.

When their dance was finished they left. There was much
noise from the audience.

Then a thin young man swayed on to the stage, took the
microphone in his hands and sang a sexual funny song.

'Who is that?' asked Carla, turning to Lewis.

'Our waiter, darling,' whispered Lewis; 'all the performers
are waiters, too. Isn't it exciting?'

Carla said nothing. Lewis looked at Holton. There was
little light in the room and he couldn't make out his expression. Holton was sitting motionless, one hand on the
table, one hand touching Carla's.

Their waiter was so well received that he sang another
song.

More dancers appeared. This time they were real women
and the men who came out with them were dressed as men.
They did a serious near-ballet but, because they didn't know
how to dance very well and because they didn't particularly
care, the dance was funny and Holton laughed. Lewis and
Carla didn't laugh : for different reasons.

Suddenly in the middle of the dance a voice off stage
announced loudly, 'Jerry!' and a girl dressed in a fake tiger
skin ran on to the stage. The audience whistled and stamped
and a table of girls near the stage applauded hysterically.
The girl's face was square and smooth and hard, without
expression. Her body was strong and slim and startlingly
white. One shoulder and most of one breast were bare.

She moved in a stylized jungle fashion among the other
dancers who ran from her, simulating fear as they did.

Finally she was left alone on the stage. She danced then, showing as much of her hard white body as she could. Her face never changed expression, however. She always looked straight ahead without smiling, her square face rigid.

And, at last, as a climax, she unfastened the tiger skin and with a quick gesture pulled it off and for a moment let the audience see her white hard body. Then the lights went off and she disappeared as the women in the audience shrieked their delight and the men, catching some of the hysteria, applauded loudly.

The lights came on again and the stage was empty. The band played uncompelling music. 'What,' asked Lewis, turning to Holton, 'did you think of her? Isn't she a perfect savage?'

'No, I don't think she is,' said Holton seriously. 'I don't think she was good at all, did you?'

'Why, yes, I thought she had something. A certain . . . how shall I say . . . banked fire?'

'I agree with Bob,' said Carla. 'I don't think she's a savage; I don't think she's natural.'

'Just prejudice,' said Lewis lightly, gesturing with his hand. 'Just prejudice; anyway, the girls here love her.' He pointed to a table of women. The dancer, wearing a dressing-gown now, was sitting on the lap of one.

Holton chuckled.

'What amuses you?' asked Lewis but Holton wouldn't answer him.

Carla told them of a similar dancer in Paris. As she talked the lights went off in the room and the band began to play. Suddenly a spotlight was turned upon the stage and the room became quiet as the people waited to see the thing they had heard of, the thing they had come to see.

Softly the orchestra played.

A boy with blond curling hair and a smooth white face walked on to the stage, turned his back on the audience, and hung a round silver moon from a hook attached to the low ceiling. He stood back a moment, looking at the moon, and then, satisfied that it was right, he stepped off the small stage and sat down on a bench near the wings.

The silver moon shone dully, dominating the stage and the room. In the middle of the room there was a mask : a painted mask, enticing, sexual, ambiguous, a youth or a woman. From this mask long veils of pink and blue silk quivered gently, stirred by the now-excited breathing of the audience. They watched this mask, and watching, waited for the dance to begin.

A voice came startlingly into the room from a loud-speaker. Said the voice : 'We take great pride in introducing the star of our show, the one and only Hermes de Bianca. To the music of a Tchaikovsky concerto he will do a dance symbolic of the struggles between the material and the spiritual natures of man. Introducing MR HERMES DE BIANCA !'

The band began to play the concerto. More lights, multi-coloured lights, were turned upon the stage. The veils of the moon fluttered and Hermes de Bianca entered.

A long sigh came from the audience as he appeared and began to dance.

He wore a thin silk costume, mysterious and black with flowing sleeves. He was fat, not grossly fat like a man, but rather the plump voluptuousness of an old belle; his skin shone white through the semi-transparent costume.

His hips were heavy and feminine. His hands and feet were tiny; he was very proud of them, for he gestured with his hands and pirouetted on the tips of his dainty feet. His breasts were the breasts of a woman.

Methodically he danced. With an obscene grace he moved about the stage, moved like a yielding woman exulting in her passivity.

His face :

There are the faces of men and there are the faces of women and there are also the faces of children, but this was yet another face.

The skin was smooth and silken-looking. The face was beautiful : his eyes were widened with paint and across the upper eyelids rows of shining, diamond-like stones were glued, making his slightest expression glitter in the light.

As he danced he would touch his hair from time to time, using the most common of feminine gestures. His hair was dark and oiled, with an artificial peak over the forehead. And, most striking of all, streaks of grey had been painted at the temples.

The music then became sad and, as it did, his dance became slower, more sensual. His wide painted mouth was never still, always working, always moist, the lips never without expression; now parted, showing desire, now petulant, now commanding, always enticing young men to love.

He moved with great lightness, handling his heaviness gracefully as he advanced upon the moon, making love to the mask.

Then, as the music became louder, more compelling, he whirled and twisted among the veils of the moon, wrapping himself in them, surrendering to the mask, approaching and retreating, always attracted to the painted mask.

But, finally, he was the one conquered, the one who surrendered, the passive one. And he stood there, the sounds of music all about him, engulfing him, his back arched, his head thrown back and his plump white stomach shuddering beneath the dark material of his costume.

And then, as the music reached a climax, he whirled in the centre of the stage, violent, obscene in a desire to be possessed.

The music stopped.

There was silence in the room – no sound save the unheard thundering of many quick-beating hearts. The ones who understood were too moved to speak and the ones who did not understand were embarrassed and sickened, aware of their danger and afraid.

He bowed to the audience now, his moist red mouth smiling brilliantly, the mouth of an actress awaiting applause. The applause came, destroying the silence in the room, creating another less frightening mood, replenishing his ego.

Smiling, he walked in triumph off the stage.

The lights were turned on at last and the orchestra played a popular song.

The boy took down the silver moon and the painted mask and as he walked away he took the reality of the dream with him and couples began to dance on the stage where Hermes de Bianca had danced. Yet as they danced, close to one another, there was a certain fear within each of them, an uncertainty and a dread.

'What do you think of that?' asked Lewis.

He was breathing quickly, Carla noticed. His face was flushed and he was excited, more excited that she had thought he could possibly be.

'It is very . . . erotic,' she said, knowing how inadequate that word was.

Holton was sweating when she turned to ask him what he thought. He looked angry.

'Did you like it, Bob?' she asked.

'No, I didn't,' he said. He took out his handkerchief and dried his face. 'Christ, but it's hot in here. Why don't we go?'

'In a moment,' said Lewis, now recovered. 'You must meet dear Hermes. I'll go back stage and get him.' He stood up, looked around the room to see if he were being watched; then, satisfied that he was, he went back stage.

'You don't care for this?' Carla asked.

'I guess I don't. I never saw anything like this before. I used to hear a lot of stories but I didn't think there were really such places.'

'There are many a lot worse,' said Carla. 'Of course I'm used to it. You see my husband is . . .'

He smiled. 'I guess you were right about not coming here.'

'You don't regret it?'

'It's interesting.'

'I think it was a very good idea for you to see something of this world. Perhaps you can understand me better now, knowing that I'm living with people like these, married to a person like Lewis.'

He frowned and looked very serious and she was happy to see him concerned. 'Can't you leave him, can't you leave Bankton?'

'Where would I go? He's a charming person and I like him. I'd have to find someone else before I could leave.'

'Yes,' he said, not understanding her, 'I see what you mean.'

George *Robert* Lewis returned leading Hermes, still in costume, by the hand.

Everyone was polite. Hermes lisped that he was glad to meet them and he shook hands squashily with both Holton and Carla. Then they sat down at the table.

Lewis was excited. 'You know Hermes has made the most dreadfully big decision? He's going to Rome!' Trumpets did not blow at that moment in the band; they should have, though.

Carla was puzzled. 'You mean he's going to Italy?'

'No, darling, he's becoming a Roman Catholic. Isn't it the most thrilling thing!'

'I suppose so,' she said. 'I used to be a Catholic myself.'

'What happened?' asked Hermes in a lisping little girl's voice.

'I seemed to've got out of the idea. I married a Protestant, of course.'

'What a pity,' murmured Hermes, looking at Holton admiringly; 'I think it's the only answer, really the only answer. Almost everyone I know is going over to Rome so there must be *something* in it.'

'Perhaps there is,' said Carla. 'I think in Italy we take the Church too much for granted.'

'I do wish,' said Lewis, 'that I could get interested in it. There seems to be such a rush for rosaries today. But I'm dreadfully afraid I'm just a hedonistic pagan.' He put his hand on Hermes' plump little hand. 'I've always felt that somewhere there is a faith that I could grasp on to.' With his other hand he took a drink out of his recently filled glass. 'Sometimes one feels so lost, so homeless. I think there must always be a womb-longing in each of us, a desire to go back where we came from. I used to think that art was enough but I suppose I was wrong because I never had much real satisfaction from it. Carla here will say it is love that gives us a reason, but I don't think so. I've always been in love. Occasionally with my own image, I must admit, but there *have* been others. No, I never got much out of love. Hermes here has his dancing, but I don't think that was enough for him either . . .'

'Perhaps you've never given enough of yourself to another person,' said Carla.

'Vampire,' chuckled Lewis. 'Our identities are the only real things we have in this shadowy world.' He was in good form now and he was becoming drugged with his own facility. 'No, we must try to obtain a faith, or at least a medium, to carry out our search for immortality, or should I say perpetuation? Women, normal women, seem to have less fear of death because they have the function of child-bearing. They are able to experience their own perpetu-ation; and in their primitive way they feel a part of all man-kind and there are no real mysteries for them, no need of logic. But man is different. The act of procreation is a pleasure and not painful and, therefore, he does not observe that in that function his own image is mirrored through eternity. He turns then to art (the sensitive talented man, I mean now) and in making pictures or books, playing at creation, he hopes to survive death but he is never really con-vinced : at best he is hypnotized, he is drugged by his art and in desperation he tries to make meaning out of his own creations : playthings, in reality. And so he finds himself in the end with chisel and mallet in his hands making a statue and no nearer perpetuation, closer only to death.'

'How beautiful!' exclaimed Hermes. 'But that's why we all have to go to Rome.'

'Perhaps that's the answer.' He began to speak again, his flat voice rising and falling without emotion in it. Carla looked at Holton questioningly. He nodded.

'Bob and I have to go now,' she said.

'Oh, you must stay a little longer,' he pleaded.

'We really have to go,' said Holton, rising. They thanked him (Lewis insisted on paying the bill) and said good-bye. George *Robert* Lewis was still talking to Hermes as they left.

ELEVEN

'How cool it is!' said Carla, as they walked along the street. 'I couldn't breathe in there.'

'It was a crazy place,' said Holton, looking straight ahead as he walked, following the traffic lights. Carla occasionally drew him off the curb and into the street but he always managed to obey the green lights.

They decided to walk uptown, to walk to Times Square.

Carla felt light and happy now that Lewis had been left behind.

'I like the air in New York,' she said.

'The air?'

'It's exciting and silly and everyone is busy doing things they don't want to do but still it's stimulating.'

'I suppose so.'

She hadn't decided yet whether he tried to be non-committal or whether he had nothing to say. No, he had something to say: she was sure of that. He was shy and he felt things very much but he was afraid to say them. She remembered now that he had told her things about himself in Florence. He had told her about his parents and his life, though he hadn't told her what he wanted to do. He still would not tell her that and, if he knew, she would have to discover it.

'How long are you going to be in town?' he asked.

'I don't know. A month perhaps, I don't know. I think Bankton will be coming over soon. They're going to give him a big show here.'

'I'd like to see him.'

'He'd like to meet you, too.' She laughed. 'I might lose you to him.' She stopped herself quickly. She shouldn't have said 'lose' because they were supposed to be just casual friends; at least that was the basis he seemed to want. She mustn't frighten him. 'I don't think you'd like him,' she said easily, in control now. 'He's rather jealous and disagreeable.'

They crossed more streets, dodged more cars, bumped into more and more people and, finally, they came to Times Square.

At Forty-second street they stopped and Carla looked at the lights for a long time.

It seemed as if all the commercialism in the world had decided to concentrate itself in one place, as if by blazing coloured lights and moving signs it could justify itself.

At one end of the square a giant sign exploded colours, advertising cigarettes. Another cigarette advertisement had a man puffing smoke; it was most realistic because real smoke or something like smoke came out of his mouth. Soft drinks and chewing gum and cigarettes – all the small things – were displayed in the most magnificent manner. There was an almost religious appeal in the brightness of the lights, the cathedral-like splendour of the signs which supported countless coloured bulbs of light : everything was so large, so magnificent, so desperately appealing.

'Such wonderful strength,' murmured Carla, 'so much misguided energy.'

'It's very nice to look at,' said Robert Holton, speaking self-consciously for America.

They stood pressed against a building while hundreds of people pushed by them in a thick stream. Carla studied the lights, mesmerized by their colours : red passionate ones and glittering greens, blue and yellow glowing, and moving figures; they even had the lights turn on and off in such a fashion that silhouetted men appeared to dance and animated animals had adventures. The lights were most splendid and nowhere in the world was so much grandeur hung against the sky. Carla watched the lights.

Yellow taxicabs clattered by them and everyone moved quickly. Everyone had at least a destination and that was a hopeful sign. She didn't care to think what their destinations might be.

She looked at the buildings and saw that they were not tall. They looked like buildings in Paris or London. Squat and dirty and rather Victorian : the buildings were most ordinary but there was so much light over them, against them, all around them that they became as insubstantial as theatre props.

The movie houses which filled the lower parts of most of the buildings of the square had the most light. Their marquees rippled and glittered with names. Large posters were hung wherever there was no electricity. People moved in constant streams into the movies while other people, as constantly, came out, blinking their eyes, adjusting themselves to reality.

Then there was the noise. Not a really individual noise, not like an Italian crowd, hoarse and insistent, but a roar with sharp breaks and a rhythm like an automobile engine, a noise like a discordant piece of music with rumblings of a subway train as a bass. The conversations of many people made a sound as soothing and as natural as the sea but the mechanical things made sharp overtones, set the rhythm of Times Square and of many lives.

Slowly Carla and Robert Holton allowed themselves to become a part of the current of people, gliding with them towards the north end of the square.

First of all were the young adventurers : boys with dark skins and dark clever eyes, dressed in the spirit of the jazz they had made their own without understanding. Looking for sex, they walked together in groups, talking in whining voices, unpleasant nasal voices.

Young girls with bleached blonde hair that looked untidy and unclean walked in twos together, looking for men. Their well-formed bodies with tight breasts moved self-consciously as they walked on awkward high heels. They laughed too loudly, giggled too much and stared at sailors.

The couples were the happiest-looking of all. They always walked with wonder in their faces, conscious of each other as they walked through all the light and sound.

Old men in dirty clothes moved slowly, looking for cigarette butts. This was not new to them; they had known the square before and found it good hunting though not as congenial as quiet places. They had stopped looking for sex : only cigarette butts.

Cripples and bums sang songs and rattled tin cups. It was hard to tell what they were looking for besides charity. Perhaps they had stopped their long search. Carla was sorry for them.

Hot stale air rushed out of the theatre lobbies and from the bars and restaurants; stale air rushed upward from the subway ventilators in the sidewalk. The cool night was defeated by the city, even the darkness had been defeated for it was as light as day, as light as day and much prettier and more exciting.

'What a place !' said Carla. 'So *much* is here. Is this the dream Lewis was talking about?'

'Maybe.'

'I think,' said Carla, laughing, 'this is the peak of your civilization.'

'Probably; it's the sign of the century.'

'But there will be other centuries.' And they thought of other centuries when they would not be alive and they tried to see the square in future years – if the square survived with the dream.

Outside the Bijou Theatre Marjorie Ventusa stood, trying to make up her mind if she wanted to see her favourite actress suffer. Marjorie liked pictures that made her cry. She wasn't sure, however, if she wanted to cry tonight.

Mrs Merrin had been quite pleasant that evening when Marjorie left and this made her feel good. She stood now, undecided, Times Square all around her. She often faced the high prices of the square to see new movies. She liked crowded places because she felt happy with a lot of people around her.

She stood beside the box office, warmed by the air from the theatre. The sight of all the people and lights made her feel secure as though she were not really alone, for she identified herself with every couple that passed by. She had no envy.

Marjorie was about to go into the movie when she saw Robert Holton crossing a street on the other side of the square. She had a sudden impulse to call him, to make herself heard over the hundreds of people. Then she saw that he was not alone. She saw that he was with a dark pretty girl : a woman from the world where he lived. Marjorie Ventusa watched him as he walked with this person across the street. Then, on the other side, she lost him. He had disappeared with the dark woman.

The square had changed now and the lights were cruel. The noises became oppressive and she felt shut out of the lives of the people who passed her.

Marjorie Ventusa grabbed her black patent-leather handbag close to her and, controlling herself, she walked along the square. She walked slowly, allowing others to push by her. She passed in front of many movie houses and many bars. There was a great noise all around her, harsh voices and much laughing. She hated the laughing the most. Two young girls were stopped by two sailors in front of her and they spoke together in the light of a red neon sign. The sailors said something and the girls laughed. Quickly Marjorie Ventusa walked by them.

A group of boys were standing in a blue light and they were laughing in their harsh changing voices. She wished they would stop. Looking downward, she walked through the crowd, no longer with it.

Marjorie Ventusa was the centre now of laughing people and her eyes were dazzled by changing lights.

Finally, out of breath, and at the northern end of the square, she stopped and pressed against a building. She looked back at the places she had just left and she was tired.

. A stout little man was staring at her. He was trying to figure out what she was and what he might dare do. She looked at him with disgust, but he was not bothered by this and, thinking her a whore, he separated himself from the crowd and came over to where she stood. He leaned against the building a few feet from her. Slowly, calmly he took a package of cigarettes out of his pocket. He turned to her now, offering her a cigarette.

'Want a smoke?'

She shook her head. 'No thanks.'

He took one himself and lighted it. He inhaled to show how calm he was and then he said, 'You want to walk maybe?'

'No,' she said furiously, comparing him with Robert Holton. 'I don't want to walk with you.' She turned away from him and went quickly towards the nearest movie. Without once looking back she bought a ticket. As she gave the ticket to the man at the door she heard the stout man whistle as he walked past the theatre.

Setting her face, she walked into the marble and gold lobby. She walked, conscious of a thousand non-existent eyes watching her back.

Then she entered the darkened hall of the movie. On the screen two characters, simulating love, were laughing loudly. Marjorie Ventusa was trapped.

Caroline and Jim Trebling had been giggling all evening. Caroline had never known anyone quite so amusing as Trebling. He had no respect for anything; at least, no respect for the things most people did. He made fun of her office and her job and he was pleasant as he did it; not bitter as so many people were.

He had suggested that they visit Times Square and go dancing in one of the large dance halls there. She had tried to talk him into going some place more expensive but he had said that he didn't have the money and that as long as you danced somewhere that was all that counted.

From Fifth Avenue they walked along Forty-Seventh Street until, finally, they came to the square. Trebling blinked.

'It's the damnedest sight! I don't think it can compare with L.A. but there really is something wonderful about it.'

Caroline regarded the square without much emotion. She had seen it all her life. 'I think it's too crowded,' she said finally, wishing that he had decided to take her to a better place, a place with a big name, one she could talk about later.

He stood, however, staring at the lights; then he lowered

his eyes from the lights and looked at the people. She noticed now that he looked at people a great deal. Even when they were talking he always stared at people as though there was something wrong with them.

'Why're you looking around all the time?' asked Caroline. 'I don't understand you at all. I don't think they like being stared at.'

'What?' He hadn't been listening to her. 'Why do I . . . stare? I just like to look at them and see what they're so busy rushing around for.'

'Don't you know?'

'No, do you?'

'Well . . .' She hesitated, uncertain of her meaning, uncertain of what they were talking about.

He laughed. She admired his way of telling when she couldn't understand him; he never really embarrassed her by trying to talk over her head as some men tried to do : not that they really could, of course. She was an American woman and just as smart as any man. Caroline stood there looking at the square with Trebling who had just laughed and saved her from embarrassment; Caroline stood erect and sure of herself and her emancipation, her arm in his.

Then, without speaking, he led her across the middle of the square. It was dazzling to cross between the many lights. Caroline liked the colours. They seemed rather cozy to her. Times Square was in many ways her symbol of home. It was no longer interesting because home is never interesting but she liked it still.

'Look at all the movie houses,' he said when they had got over on the other side. 'There's so much of everything But it's dirty. It's all awfully dirty.'

'Is it?' Caroline had not thought of that. Perhaps the square was not very clean but how could it be? There were always so many people coming to be impressed or depressed by it.

'Bob used to talk a lot about this part of town, about Broadway. I think he used to like it a lot,' said Trebling.

'Is that right?'

'Oh, sure. He was a playboy during the war.'

Caroline was surprised but not very interested. 'He sure's changed a lot,' she said. 'He's a nice fellow and I know you think a lot of him but he's a little dull . . . now, anyway.'

'I think,' said Trebling, 'that people sometimes feel they have to change to protect themselves. He's just making a new life now.'

'He's certainly making a dull one.'

'Not if it's what he wants.'

'Imagine working in an office if you could do something else!'

'What about yourself?'

Caroline flushed; she found herself becoming so much involved with Trebling's personality that she had begun to lose her own in his: she had begun to think that she was as free as he was or, rather, as he felt he was. She had to retrace now; she must go back into herself. 'I can't do anything else,' she said. 'That's all I know – working in an office.'

'You could get married.'

'I suppose I could.' Purposely she left it at that. He didn't ask her anything else. They watched the square.

Caroline was conscious of odours, too conscious of them. There were a great many unpleasant odours in the square: beer and cigarette smoke and exhaust; perfume and sweat and stale air from theatres and subways; food cooking – hot dogs, hamburgers, popcorn and peanuts. She got a little dizzy just breathing.

'Come on, Jim,' she said, 'let's go find the dance hall.'

They walked together along the crowded streets and as they walked he told her wonderful stories of freedom that were not true but still very interesting; and she thought him the most fascinating man she knew and not at all like his dull friend Robert Holton.

At last they came to a dance hall. As much as she liked the glitter of the square it was a relief to go inside the red-upholstered, mirror-walled dance hall where the only odours were of perfume and cigarette smoke.

'I haven't been here for so long,' she said.

Mr Heywood came out of the theatre. He had left in the

middle of the last act. It was his personal strategy to do this because it meant that he missed the crowd and the long wait for his car to find him.

The play had been dreary and he had seen it only because a friend of his knew the girl in it. Besides, Mr Heywood did not like to go to plays alone. His wife no longer went with him and he was afraid of taking other women around with him because people talked. He did not like any men at all.

The street was almost deserted. The theatres still were full and their chaste white light signs shone cleanly into the street. Two blocks away was Times Square. He could just barely make out the coloured sign of a soft drink bottle. He shuddered as he thought of soft drinks.

He stood in front of the theatre, the light from the marquee shining dramatically down upon him. He would stand here now without moving until his waiting chauffeur saw him and took him away. To his left he heard the sound of a motor starting. He did not look to his left. He merely stood now, self-contained and passive, waiting.

His car stopped in front of him. The chauffeur got out, opened the door and said something to him and Mr Heywood said something to the chauffeur and an understanding was reached. Mr Heywood got into the car and the chauffeur drove down the street into the square and towards home.

Mr Heywood shrank from the lights that suddenly made the inside of his car as colourful as a rainbow. He tried not to look out the window at the square but it was impossible not to look. His eyes were drawn by the force of the lights and he looked out finally.

All the cheapness he hated was in the square. The people of whom he was terrified moved all about him now. The noises he hated to hear and the lights he hated to see intruded. He shuddered and wondered if he was going to be sick.

Finally they left the square.

He felt much better now that they were in the quieter darker places of the city. Mr Heywood was lonely now. He had always been lonely and it was his personal sadness. He wished that he were young. It was impossible to be lonely when one was young. He wished that he were Robert Holton.

Carla and Holton stopped to rest at the northern end of the square. They stood upon a small island of concrete surrounded by avenues. A red light shone across Holton's face giving him a sinister expression. Carla laughed.

'What's so funny?'

'Your face . . . you look like Mephisto.' He smiled and stepped out of the red light and stood beside her.

'What do you think of it now?' asked Holton as they stood on their island, watching.

'The things I've always thought. It's very brilliant. It is a . . . production.'

'Everyone comes to see it.'

'And I think it means something different to each one. It's like a work of art that way.' She paused and added. 'It is a work of art.'

'An unfriendly one, though.'

She shrugged. 'Art doesn't have to be friendly. To me all this bad taste is very alive and malicious.' She was going to say more but she was not sure of her English. The language she had learned had been literary and she was occasionally conscious of not speaking ordinary words. Holton had not been listening, though. Caught in the magic she had performed upon the square, he was melting into it, his eyes fixed on the effect and not the details.

'What a place to make a decision,' he said firmly, turning to look at her.

'A decision?' She was not sure of him now; not sure of the magic. 'What sort of decision?'

'I'll tell you later.'

'If you like.' She could see that he was not ready to talk to her yet. The signs were good, though. He was returning.

Arm in arm they deserted their concrete island. They crossed the street and stood for a moment on the edge of the square, looking back at the lights.

'Where do you want to go?' asked Holton.

'Back to my hotel,' she said, not looking at him.

'Shall I go with you?'

'Do you want to?' She noticed that one of the largest signs had several dead lights in it.

'Of course I want to,' he said.

She was very happy then. The bridge was completed.

'Shall we walk? It's not far.' He nodded. They left the bright square and walked northward, not speaking. The bridge was not yet strong.

TWELVE

They stood a moment in the grey heavily carpeted corridor. The hotel was an expensive one and this was the first time Robert Holton had been inside it.

'I'm down here,' said Carla, taking a key out of her bag. She led him down the corridor.

She stopped, unlocked the door, and they went inside.

'In America you always try to make everything look expensive,' she said. 'But I like this room.'

'Looks like Hollywood,' said Holton. Carla looked about her and agreed. The walls were dull green and the ceiling white. The furniture was low and modern and there was much glass in the room : mirrors and glass-topped tables. Two large windows looked out on Central Park. At the left was the doorway to the bedroom.

'Bankton must have a lot of money,' murmured Holton. Carla smiled. 'No, I have, but that's not important. Sit down over there, Bob.' She motioned to a white couch by the window. 'Would you like something to drink?'

'If you want one.'

While she fixed his drink she would be able to think of the right thing to say. She felt constrained still and her heart was beating rapidly. She prepared the drink deliberately and, satisfied that it was right, she turned and walked over to him. 'Here you are.' Then she sat down beside him.

They looked out at the city. Carla sat straight on the edge of the couch, her eyes fixed on the tall buildings. She was conscious of Holton's slow breathing beside her. The silence was becoming difficult; then he picked up his glass and ice clattered and the silence broke.

'Tell me,' she said, sitting back in the couch, 'what do you do during the days? What does a broker do?'

He opened his coat and relaxed. 'Not much, I'm afraid. I get all sorts of statistical books and I make out reports from them. It's pretty dull.'

'How long are you going to have to do that?'

'I don't know . . . a year maybe. I think Mr Heywood – he was the fellow we met at the party – I think he's going to move me out in the selling end.'

'You would like that?'

'It means more money and it's going to be my career.'

'That's right; it's going to be your career.'

Holton crossed his legs, using the movement to give himself time to think. Carla waited, watching him.

'Are you going to live in Florence?' he asked finally.

This was not going at all well, she thought. 'I think I may live there part of the year. I think I shall travel first.'

'Where? Where do you want to go?'

'Some place in the Near East, some place like the *Arabian Nights* – you've read it, haven't you?'

'I read it once.'

'I always wanted things to be like that, to be enchanted.'

'And you've been disappointed?'

She nodded. 'Sometimes I've been very disappointed but, you see, sooner or later it's all right. I've great faith in things being right.'

'You're a curious girl,' he said. He looked at her and she could see her own face twice reflected in his eyes. 'You don't,' he said, 'really like Bankton, do you?'

The words were making the proper patterns now. She turned so that he could see all her face when she spoke. 'Yes, I like him very much but I don't love him. I can't love anyone without having it complete, without having . . . the other thing.'

'What we had.'

'Yes, what we had.' She felt that now he was coming back again.

'It was so long ago, wasn't it?' She wasn't sure now that he was coming back : 'so long ago.'

'I've remembered it,' she said. 'It doesn't seem long ago to me.'

'I don't mean that,' he said. 'I meant that . . . well . . . so much has happened to us since then. You've been married and I left the army . . .'

'We're not much different, are we?' She looked out the window now and watched different lights go out in the tall buildings; for each light that went out, though, someone else turned on another. 'You know,' she said, concentrating on the lights, 'you know you were really the first for me.'

He was awkward now. 'Yes, I guess I was. I didn't . . .'

'There were probably a lot of others for you in Europe. You know, I haven't really wanted any man since then.'

This had to surprise; she wanted this to be her strongest weapon. She looked at him now. He had put down his drink and he was looking at her.

'Is that true?'

She nodded. 'I don't know why I shouldn't tell you. I couldn't keep from telling you.' She tried not to look at him.

'You mean what happened to us in Italy was the only time . . .?' He was confused.

She turned then and looked at him, at the troubled eyes and the boy's mouth. 'My dear, when something means a lot to you I think it's hard to take a substitute. You see, I made an object for myself. I was upset when you left, naturally, because you'd become my object. I never heard from you and so I married Bankton in London. I never lost my object, though. It never changed.'

'I'm sorry,' he said.

Carla smiled. 'I understand it now. You had so many women and I was only one. I think that's all right, I think that's natural. I hoped you might have felt the way I did. One always wants to be loved and it's not easy to find a lover. I never had another man – not because I couldn't, but because I didn't want to. I was waiting all that time, hoping to see *you* again.' She had said everything now. He had listened and there was nothing else she could do.

He ran his hands through his hair. 'I was very close to you,' he said.

'I thought you were.' She was waiting.

'You're right, there were lots of others, but I don't think I loved any of them.'

'No one at all?'

He didn't answer. He stood up and walked across the room. Then he came back and stood looking down at her.

'I don't know what to say. We were very close once and then I came back here and made myself forget everything about Europe, everything that had had happened to me there.

'It hasn't been easy to do. The only way I could get by, though, was to do what I'm doing : become a broker. I can't be the way I was; I can't afford it. Of course I can still have all the girls I want and I can have a good time. I suppose I can fall in love sometime . . . again, but I have to be a conventional person and I don't mind.

'Tonight those people were examples of freedom . . .'

She interrupted him. 'Not really freedom, self-indulgence perhaps.'

'Whatever it is, they call it being free. I don't want that. I couldn't have that kind anyway because I'm not talented; I don't do anything well and I know it.'

'You can be a free person, though.'

'How?'

She sighed. 'I've already told you and you already know. You can love.'

'You think that's the answer?'

'I don't know any other. It's been important to me.'

He sat down beside her, sat close to her. 'I don't know if I could love someone,' he said. 'I don't know if I could love you the way you'd want.'

'You can,' said Carla. 'You can do whatever you want.'

His hand touched hers. She sat very straight then, her eyes on the window, on the white lights. He put his arm around her shoulders and kissed her and he closed her eyes upon the lights outside.

For a long time they were like that on the couch. Then they separated and stood up, self-conscious and shy, newly discovered. He motioned with his hand towards the bedroom. She nodded and they went into the bedroom together and met finally in the middle of the bridge.

Robert Holton held Carla from him at arm's length and looked at her. She was pretty, at this moment quite beautiful, her face white and her greenish eyes glittering.

'I've been waiting, Bob,' she said. 'I've waited such a long time.' He pulled her to him then, her body against his. A part of him was given up entirely to making love but another part was still detached, still watching.

He helped her to undo her dress. Modestly now, with the reserve of strangers, they stood back to back as they undressed.

She was beautiful and he had forgotten that. She was not really pale: her skin was gold. She was slim and cleanly made and her breasts were small. They faced each other and looked at each other, the detached, the lonely part of himself memorizing every detail of her.

Carla walked slowly towards him and touched his shoulder. Tears were in her eyes.

'What's the matter?' he asked.

She shook her head and smiled : nothing was the matter now.

He took her slowly then, pressing her against his body gently, every nerve vibrating in both of them; hearts beating quickly.

They stood like this in the middle of the room; then she broke away and walked over to the bed and pulled the cover down.

'Turn out the light, Bob,' she whispered. It was a ceremony now : neither of them spoke out loud in the presence of the miracle taking place. He turned out the light. The room was dark except for the lighted dots of windows in the buildings opposite and, over the buildings, like unorganized window lights, cold stars shone clearly.

He turned and walked to the bed. Carla lay on her back, her arms behind her head. He got in beside her and they lay there together, not speaking, hardly breathing, and he felt the blood pounding in his head while, next to him, Carla was shivering, was waiting. He turned over on his side, barely touching her.

They did not speak now. Words were discarded and no surface was needed. Instinct guided them finally, made them a separate world together; there was only a dream existence outside themselves.

And Robert Holton became the lover and ceased to be himself; his detached awareness was, for the time, submerged and forgotten.

He ran his hands over her, feeling the smooth skin of her shoulders, her thighs . . . They kissed and began the act of completion.

To Holton it became a battle and a surrender, a taking and a giving, it became a fusion. He was no longer himself, he was enlarged; a giant in a world of giant sensations. He was no longer alone or incomplete.

Then the rhythm was found and the wild twistings and strugglings stopped. He was conquering now and, in the conquering, giving.

He entered her and to the rhythm of their fast-beating hearts, with a rush of sound like wind in his ears, he discovered the single world. Lights whirled inside his head, behind his eyes : they came in series – circles of sharp lights.

He was choking then, barely breathing, able only to cough and gasp. Sweat covered him; his hands clutched at her shoulders as though they were the only remaining solidity in a world rapidly disintegrating into sensations and fast-moving lights and a quick wind.

There was no time now. There was no memory. There was no reason. The struggle stopped and the moment came like fire.

Carla's face was buried in his shoulder; she stiffened and then became relaxed, the battle finished and won.

Like fire it came and the wonder was achieved; a world was glimpsed and lost in a moment. Then, tide-like, the emotion stopped and withdrew. The ecstasy was gone and only two people were left in its wake, left on a high shore, exhausted, shipwrecked.

Robert Holton lay for a moment upon Carla's still body,

supporting himself with his elbow so that he would not crush her; he breathed deeply, taking in the air with great sobs. Beneath him Carla was quiet, at peace, her shuddering stopped.

He kissed her very gently then and they separated, without words; they lay quietly side by side, touching each other, yet apart, the trace of their fire still inside of them, and exhaustion brought with it no sadness, no loneliness.

Robert Holton put his arm under her head; then he looked out the window, looked at the real stars, not nearly as bright as the ones in his head, the ones they had made together.

Silence and darkness protected them.

Part of his mind became detached again and he saw himself in relation to the world. He saw himself in a darkened room of a large hotel, lying exhausted beside the wife of a painter. He frowned in the dark and he fought the vision of the outer world.

Carla moved her hand over his chest, twisting the hairs; he felt a spasm of tenderness shake him and he took her and held her close to him. This was the moment when he felt he was not alone, felt that he was not a single particle lost in a void. The half of them lost in the womb had been regained and he was finally complete : he was God and earth and other stars, so great was this fusion.

They slept quietly in each other's arms. They slept unaware of time for they *were* time.

Carla woke first. She gave a start and Robert Holton opened his eyes, wondered where he was; then he saw Carla beside him, saw a vague figure by the light of stars.

'*Caro mio,*' she murmured, saying the first words either had spoken.

'Darling,' he whispered.

'It's so perfect,' she said and he put her head on his shoulder again. Then they were still, looking at the uncertain outline of their bodies on the whiteness of the bed.

He felt her smooth legs. They were cool, like dreams half-remembered.

'I love you,' she whispered into his ear, 'so much more than you know.'

148

He kissed her for answer and his detached self almost fused with hers, almost made a union, almost died and made him free.

Carla turned on the light. It was two o'clock and they had been asleep for almost an hour.

Robert Holton lay quiet on the bed, his eyes closed, his breathing regular, one arm over his forehead as though to defend himself. She leaned and kissed him lightly, then she got out of bed and went into the bathroom.

Her face shocked and pleased her. 'How depraved I look,' she murmured to herself. Her face was glowing and her eyes shone and glittered. There were red marks on her white skin. His beard had scratched her and made her usually white face pink. With a sudden gesture she swept her hair back out of her face, held her dark curling hair captive.

Holton appeared behind her then and he put his arms around her waist and kissed the back of her neck. She shuddered and closed her eyes. She could not look at light with so much inward light behind her eyes. They stood like that. Then he let her go. They looked at each other : two people now, so recently a single world.

'Happy?' she asked.

He nodded. 'I've never had it like this before,' he said. 'It never meant as much to me as this.'

They walked back into the bedroom and sat down side by side on the bed. Modestly Holton drew the sheet over their laps. They sat quietly without speaking, their bare arms around each other. When Carla looked at the window she could no longer see stars and lighted windows; she could see only their reflection on black glass.

'What are you thinking?' he asked and she saw that he'd been watching her.

'Nothing, Bob. I don't think all the time, you know. I was only feeling.'

'Feeling what?'

She smiled. 'Feeling all the world.'

'I think I felt that, too . . . to live in a big way . . .'

'Yes, I know.' She sighed. 'You have to break all your little patterns. You have to expand now.'

But there was resistance to this. 'I don't see why you can't have everything and still have that, too.'

'No, everything must be the richest and the fullest. Have you that?'

He stretched, the muscles moving under white skin. 'Maybe it is; I don't know.' He stook her then and they fell back together on to the bed. For several minutes they were together and then he rolled over on his side. She opened her eyes.

'What's the matter, Bob?' she asked.

'I don't know,' he said. He was looking at her, his dark hair in his eyes. He pushed it back.

'You're not sad?'

'No.' He ran his hands over her hips. 'I was only wondering what's to happen next. You'll go back to Europe.'

She had been waiting for this. She had been waiting for him to ask this. Now she could say what she felt but the words did not come easily. 'I don't have to go back,' she said. 'I can stay here as long as I like.'

'Then your husband'll come over here.'

'I can leave him.'

He shook his head. 'I couldn't marry you.'

She was lost. She was falling now. It seemed as if the room had become cold and foreign and she had come to a hostile country. There was no longer an answer to make : the answer had been made. She tried not to let her face show what she felt.

'Why couldn't you marry me?'

'I haven't any money.'

'I have.'

'I wouldn't want that. You wouldn't want to be married to a broker and live in New York.'

'Why do you have to be a broker?'

He sighed then and saw for the first time that he was the one trapped, the one who would not escape. 'What else can I do?' he said.

'You can break with all this.' She was fighting.

'But what could I do? I have to do something. I have to be something.'

'Why do you have to be something? Why do you have to do things that you don't want, that make you unhappy?'

'Everyone has to. Besides, I'm not sure that I am unhappy.' She was defeated at that moment. The dream she had been fashioning disappeared and there were no traces of it left, only a lingering sadness and an open wound.

He went on talking and she answered him but there was nothing left for either of them to discuss.

Then after a while they both stopped talking. They sat side by side looking out the window, or rather looking at themselves reflected in the black mirror. Holton turned out the light and Carla was able to see the stars again.

'That was funny, wasn't it?' chuckled Holton.

'What? What was funny?'

'Lewis tonight and all those people talking about religion and art.'

'I don't think it was funny; I think it was sad.'

'Why sad?'

'They were lost, I think. Just like us, Bob.'

She could feel him looking at her. 'Are you?' he asked softly.

She would not let herself cry. She would not give way. She would have to be strong now. Her voice carefully controlled, she said, 'No more than you. We would be complete, I think.'

'I think we could,' he said and she knew that he felt nothing the way she did. Carla had the feeling of coming into a stranger's house expecting friends, expecting familiar things. She was with an unknown, a man who did not feel what she did.

'I had hoped,' said Carla, 'that we could.' She was going to be accurate in what she said. She used each word like the cut of a knife to sever the relationship, to kill her own love. 'I don't think we can now. You want to live a certain life. You want what you know and though you don't like it you think it's the safe thing. I don't understand you, I'm afraid. I've tried to see all this through your eyes. I didn't want it to be just another one, another woman. I wanted it to be important to you : it was so important to me. I think I was wrong. I think I was selfish and I'm sorry.' She wondered when her voice would break.

Then Holton tried to reconstruct at last. 'No, you don't understand. I feel very close to you. I've liked this more than any other time, more than with anyone else. But you see I can't leave what I'm doing; I couldn't live on you for the rest of my life.'

She sighed. 'That's such a superficial thing; that's all the surface. When you feel something for another person those things don't matter.'

'Someday they might. Of course I'm lonely and not very happy. You have to accept that. In a few years I'll get married and maybe that'll make it better. I could,' he was speaking slowly now, 'marry you. I could do that but you wouldn't be happy.'

'How do you know I wouldn't be happy here?'

'You're different, that's all. I can't tell you what the difference is. I don't know.'

And she couldn't tell him what the difference was. There was no way to tell.

He put his arms around her in the dark and they relaxed on the bed and she tried to give herself to the moment but she could not : too much had been given already.

'It's a temptation,' said Holton suddenly.

'What is?' They separated.

'To go to Europe with you, to live with you.'

'It could be done.'

'Maybe . . . No, it wouldn't work.'

'Why?'

'It just wouldn't be practical.'

No, she thought, it wouldn't be practical.

Then the passion came back to them and she almost forgot his withdrawal. She fell back on to the pillows, his body over hers.

He whispered in her ear, 'You know I really have to leave after this.'

'Of course you must,' said Carla, dying gently.

3

THE YELLOW WOOD

THIRTEEN

The early morning was cold and Robert Holton shivered as he left the warm lobby of the hotel. He stood outside on the sidewalk and wondered where he was. He turned to the left and walked a few steps and then he remembered the street he was on, remembered where east and west were. He turned to the right and walked rapidly towards Fifth Avenue.

The streets were almost deserted. Occasionally a taxicab would clatter by. Occasionally a tired couple looking for a room would pass him on the sidewalk. As he walked, his own footsteps made sharp regular noises on the pavement.

He came at last to a subway entrance. He breathed deeply, took a last breath of clean air and went down inside the ground.

Pale lights burned in old sockets and a sleepy Negro sat within the money-changer's booth. A sailor stood vomiting in a corner; he was very quiet about it and the Negro paid no attention to him.

Robert Holton put his nickel in the turnstile.

On the platform several people were waiting for the train. They were all tired. Another sailor had a girl and he was standing very close to her. They were both drunk and made strange little movements with their heads and hands, slow-motion movements, as though they were flying.

Robert Holton stood against an iron pillar. He felt exhausted but physically serene. He rested his head on the hard rough surface. It was pleasant to stand like this, underground.

The uptown train stopped with a jolt, the doors opened

and Robert Holton stepped into the lighted train. The doors closed and the train started again.

Everyone in the car was weary or drunk or both. Papers and cigarette butts covered the floor. A pair of dirty gloves lay at his feet, forgotten by the owner, unwanted.

Robert Holton tried to sleep but the glare of light through his eyelids was distracting. His physical exhaustion was lessening, too, and he began to feel a return of energy.

He would not think of Carla, though; he would not think of her for a little while. He would wait until he was in his room.

After a long time, after ten minutes, the train stopped at his station and he climbed out of the ground and stood on the concrete surface of the earth; a suggestion of morning was in the sky and the wind blew fresh and cold from the river. He walked to his hotel.

'Evening,' said the clerk behind the desk.

'Good evening,' said Holton.

'Is it getting colder out?'

Holton nodded. 'Probably be a real cold day tomorrow.' He walked over to the counter. 'Have I got any mail?'

'Let's see ... that's ...?'

'Holton.'

The clerk looked, then shook his head. 'No mail, Mr Holton.' He paused. 'You was in the army?'

'Yes, I was in the army.'

'So was I.' The clerk was lonely and wanted to talk and Holton was still tired and nervous and wanted to think. 'It sure is nice being out,' said the clerk.

'Yes, it's good to be out.'

'I was with the 82nd; you remember the 82nd, don't you?'

'Of course I do.'

'We had a good group of guys.'

'I know you did.'

'Nothing like being a civilian, is there?'

'No,' said Robert Holton, 'there's nothing like being out. Good night.'

'Good night.' The clerk who had been with the army was sad to see him go.

He turned the light on in his room. It was all just the same, the troubling painting and the crowded dresser. Sometimes he would come into his room and have a feeling that everything would be changed when he turned on the light, that something exciting would have happened to change his room. It was always the same, though; always the way he left it.

Holton went into the bathroom. He should take a bath; he wanted to take a bath but he was too tired. In the morning; there would be time for that in the morning.

He undressed and put on the bottom of his pyjamas; he never used the tops. Then he looked at himself in the mirror for a long time. He did not see himself in the mirror; he saw no image; rather he was trying to find an image, an explanation in the glass. But he found nothing and as he realized his failure the reflection of his face appeared in the mirror and he looked at it without interest because it was familiar and because he could see nothing behind it.

He turned and went into his room. He sat down on the bed and wondered whether he could sleep or not because his mind was uneasy. Holton turned out the lights and stretched out on his bed. He would make himself sleep; he would not think of Carla or of the day ended.

But his mind was too active now for him to sleep. He tried to hypnotize himself, tried not to hear the odd words and conversations in his ears.

He gave up finally. The barriers went down.

George *Robert* Lewis's voice sounded in his head and the clashing colours of the fairy night club glittered in his head. Lewis's voice, flat and nasal, became articulate.

'I do feel that religion is merely a substitute for the loss of a personal vision.' His sharp little laugh sounded and the words repeated themselves over and over again in Robert Holton's ear : 'loss of a personal vision . . . a vision . . . and elision . . .' The words became a refrain. The repetitions went on until Holton felt himself losing control. He was angry. He made the repetitions stop.

George *Robert* Lewis began to talk again.

'I feel that we can find some way through the morass of

157

life, some way to be serene and not sterile, not static. I think probably art is the way for the sensitive. If one has talent one can practise a medium; without talent one can appreciate.

'Love? What *does* that word mean, darling? I've tried so awfully hard to be sincere about it and I've had some delicious attempts at it. Did you ever know Philip? . . . No, of course you wouldn't have known. But as I was saying . . . what was I saying?'

Holton tried consciously to recall what Lewis had said. But when he tried to hear speeches again he could not. Lewis's voice began again, a disembodied voice speaking among colours in a place where all emotions were in a minor key.

'I think one must really barricade oneself against the world. One must retreat. Now don't tell me it's cowardly to retreat. Nothing in this world should be put on such a superficial basis as this. We are talking on different planes. That's why communication is so difficult. Every argument is true and false and can be argued rightly from either side. To have any agreement those discussing should decide right away on what plane they want to talk. On a superficial and obvious one the terms bravery and cowardice and right and wrong have a certain meaning. On a deeper plane they have different, sometimes opposite, meanings – sometimes no meaning at all.

'Well, to get back to my point, on the *deepest* level of understanding only instinct and what is natural counts. If one can't arrive at love (and so many of us, darling, haven't the capacity for it) then one must make a substitute, something to take up the sixty or seventy years one is alive. That's where art is important. I understand business men feel the same way about business, though I'm not at all sure about that.

'And then as for all this drivelling about going to Rome let me say I do feel that religion is merely a substitute for the loss of a personal vision . . .'

The sound of Lewis's voice became louder and continued until finally the voice became so loud that it ceased to be a voice and became silence.

Robert Holton wanted to sleep but there were so many things that had to be arranged first.

There was also the dream of the night before to be recalled. He would think of that later.

He remembered Jim Trebling. He thought of the days on the boat when they had talked about the future.

Against a background of sea he could recall the image of Trebling. Details were absent and he could not make out the face but he could hear the voice and he could see the ocean.

'I hate the idea of being tied down any more than I have to be. You know, Bob, we've lived the most unnatural life there is during this war. I get the feeling sometimes that we've lost a lot of time. I keep wanting to start over again.

'I might want to start my own business. I think that's not so bad : it's worse working for somebody else. It's funny but I'd just as soon never work. I'd just as soon drift the rest of my life.'

And Robert Holton had agreed. He agreed in those days.

'Of course you have to have money to loaf. Maybe if we hadn't been raised in such a sound middle-class way we could be bums but we're too used to being comfortable. No, we're too used to being comfortable. We've got to get the money first.'

Robert Holton had agreed to that, too. He had agreed to everything. He wanted to be as free as possible. At least he thought he had then. Because his friend wanted it he felt he did too. He assumed a similar identity.

Trebling had more to say and his deep laughing voice continued : 'No, we're going to have to work a little. Not much, just a little to get enough ahead. We're going to be careful though not to get bogged down, not to get too interested in working. It's dangerous to get to like it.'

Holton agreed.

'Well, Bob, get your mind on the ball. How're we going to spend that army money ? I think pottery out in California sounds easy.'

Yes, pottery was easy. Then they separated and they changed. Or perhaps only he, Holton, had changed. He'd done the easiest thing, he thought. But it was true he was entangled now for the rest of his life with Heywood and Golden; with them or another like them.

Trebling was entangled, too. Holton was pleased by that as he lay in the dark. Trebling hadn't done better. He belonged to the army now and his chances of beginning a business were slight. He might try it though; he might be able to live the way he wanted to. Holton shuddered. It would be awful to miss freedom so narrowly.

There was a problem, still unsolved : what did he want?

'You know,' said Trebling's voice, rising up out of the sea, 'you know you make things tough for yourself. You don't make up your mind.'

That wasn't true, he was always plotting; most of the time, anyway.

'You try to be like everybody else.'

He was safest when he was like the rest of them. No, that wasn't a bad thing to do; besides, he wasn't that way really. He was different from the others in the office. They sensed that. He would probably go a long way and most of them wouldn't. Perhaps he was like Heywood. That wasn't bad. Heywood was a success. *He* could be free if he liked. He had money and he could do whatever he liked.

Trebling's voice was fainter now and the sound of the sea behind it was becoming loud. 'Sure we might flop but if we don't we're just fine. I'm not worried; I'm not worried about anything except being stuck in an office and working for somebody. That's a lot to worry about, I suppose, but I'm not bothered. It's going to work out. You're a long time dead, I figure . . .'

The sea came into Holton's room then and he was whirled on the top of a wave, for a moment there was nothing but sensation. He opened his eyes in the dark and the sea was gone.

Trebling's voice was lost.

Holton turned over on his side, troubled, tired, looking for sleep. He thought of Carla. He had to think of her; there was a decision to be made.

She had been quiet when he left her in the apartment. She had not looked him in the eyes and he had been eager to leave, to escape.

Now she began to speak again. She had talked to him as he was dressing.

'I don't think it would work now. I'd hoped it would; for a long time I've thought about you, about our living together. But you don't want to.'

He had tried to deny this but he could not deny what he felt.

Her voice came back to him now, a sad thin echo; there was no vibrancy in the remembered voice. She was whispering in an empty room.

'You're going to accept a pattern and I can't stop you. I can't bring out the capacity for love in you. You have it, I know, but I'm not enough to make you aware . . .'

Again the denial and again the sad voice whispering.

'No, I was wrong to try to change your life. It's very selfish to do things for people they don't want done. I wanted you so much. You're the one I'm not supposed to have, though, and that's sad for me.'

He had talked to her then and explained that he could not take the risk of living with her, that he must be within the pattern. But he could not make any of these things sound convincing. Somehow everything got confused as he tried to explain himself to her. He tried to tell her that he did love her but that he couldn't live with her. She had listened and when he had finished she had talked again. Now her voice entered his room; it was a shadow's voice murmuring in his ear.

'I don't think I'd better see you again, Bob. It's very hard for me but I'm going to control myself. I am going to forget all the things I had dreamed about since Florence. I shall find a new object and that's a hard thing to do. It's hard to change but I will.

That was true, of course. There was also more.

She walked with him to the door; she let him go free to his chosen prison.

The little voice no longer whispered in his ear and there was nothing but silence and the beating of his heart, the slow beating of his heart.

The shade of the window fluttered in the outside wind.

Bits of light gleamed around the shade as it fluttered. Lights from signs and behind those lights, grey and massive, was the light of early morning. The room grew colder.

He got under the blanket and he closed his eyes tight and thought of nothing : thought of shapes and shadows and lights and colours and all things that comprise nothing : he could not sleep.

Robert Holton made a case for himself as he lay in the occasionally broken dark.

He had no gift. He was an average person. Perhaps not quite average, he had had many advantages. He was among the many, though. He could not make a world separate. He wished now that he had told Carla that: he could not make a world separate. He belonged to the world of all people and it was wrong to retreat from the world. He felt noble as he thought of this : it was an excellent argument and he wished that he had used it.

To have gone to live with Carla would have been a retreat from all that was right. Right? What had Lewis said about the planes of understanding? It didn't matter because Lewis was just another little fairy. He was perverted in everything. No, it was right not to live with Carla. He had to do what was expected of him.

Robert Holton built himself an argument, and as he built his barricades stronger he was aware of discontent, well-hidden beyond the barricade but still alive. Duty was important and difficult. Nothing that was right was easy. Was that true? He was becoming confused.

He had worn too many faces. He thought of the myriad faces he had been made to wear. He had been different with every person he'd ever known. This lack of consistency bothered him. In the army he had been without care, without ambition; he had been like Trebling.

With the people in the office he had been cold or warm, as they were. He had given them what they expected. He had been an actor with too many roles to play. Tonight he had played all of them for Carla and then he had become lost and he had tried to be himself and he found that he was not enough.

162

Every person saw him differently, not entirely because every person was different, but because he had also intended it to be that way. Now he did not know himself. He had no way of knowing the person behind the myriad faces.

For a moment he felt himself sinking. It was like a dream of falling. He seemed to be descending into a pit without bottom. There was no longer a Robert Holton : only a series of masks, cracked now and no longer usable, no longer convincing. He could never use one again.

He stopped falling; by an effort of will he stopped himself. Carla was gone and he was sorry. There was no one else and loneliness now crept out of the silence. He would have to build the barricades stronger and higher. He would shut loneliness out.

The masks were no longer good. Carla had helped him break them. This was to be a beginning then. He would assume an identity. He would become a decided person and he would cease to be changed by others.

Robert Holton would become a successful broker working in an office.

The decision was made and he felt secure at last. The words and thoughts that had been in his mind, troubling him, stopped abruptly. He had a magic of his own and he had used it and it worked. Now he was free. There would be no more talk of going away to Florence and living with a pretty woman who loved him and wanted him to be different. He was resolved at last. It was as simple as that. With great effort he assumed an identity and freed himself from doubt.

He stopped twisting. The fever was leaving and he was tired.

Robert Holton turned over on his stomach and took a deep breath. Soon he would be asleep. All his questions were solved – except one. There was still something to be taken care of, something not very important, but bothersome. He frowned with his eyes shut. Then he opened them and he looked across the room at the dark outline of the picture frame.

The dream.

He hadn't been able to remember the dream of the night before : the troubling, unpleasant dream. It had great significance, he knew.

His only half-conscious mind tried to remember. He kept it purposefully unawake because in this state, between sensation and memory, most dreams could be recalled.

For a long time he wondered. But he could not remember, and he went to sleep finally, exhausted, and in his mind was hidden the dream of the night before, the secret dream, the dream of death, of living. He had almost remembered.

FOURTEEN

The next day was cold, colder than the early morning had been.

Robert Holton took a bath, dressed, and went down in the elevator. He said good morning to the man at the desk who gave him a letter from his father. Then he went outside; shivering, he walked to the subway station. Without buying a paper he went down into the ground and at Wall Street he came to the surface again.

Marjorie Ventusa was glad to see him. The movie she had seen the night before had been a successful tragedy and she had wept and had been able to think about herself less tragically afterwards.

She watched him as he came into the restaurant. He went to his usual table and sat down. After he was seated she picked up a tray and walked over to him.

'Good morning, Mr Holton,' she said, and smiled.

'Hello, Marjorie. How's everything going?'

'Fine, just fine. Weather's getting cold, though.' She noticed that he had dark circles under his eyes. She tried not to think of what he might have been doing with the dark-haired girl.

'Got anything good for breakfast? I feel pretty worn out today.'

'I guess you were out late last night.'

He nodded. She couldn't stop asking now; she couldn't stop thinking about Robert Holton and the dark-haired girl.

'Probably one of those big parties, I guess.'

He nodded and said, 'Sure, one of those big parties.'

165

She was not sorry that he lied. 'We got some good sausage today,' she said.

'I'll take whatever you got . . . and black coffee.'

'Sure, I'll go get it.' She walked back to the kitchen. She frowned when she saw Mrs Merrin looking at her. She had to look serious even though she was happy. He had at least not wanted to tell her that he was out with another girl. She had made so many images of Holton and herself that she accepted an imagined closeness as real. He had not really been unfaithful this time.

She called out his order to the cook and then she fixed her snood in the steamy mirror. She had bought a dark snood and she noticed now that it made her hair look darker, look rather mysterious. It felt good to look mysterious.

His breakfast was ready and she took it out to him.

She made herself busy at the next table and she talked to him as she worked.

'You like going out to them big parties?'

'Not so much.'

'Why do you go?'

'Business, I guess. It's good to see all the big shots.'

'You're right there; you're sure right there.'

'What's that you got on your head?'

She giggled self-consciously and wished that she didn't get so silly when she was pleased. 'Just a snood. I've had it such a long time.' This was not true.

'Looks nice,' said Holton seriously, biting into a piece of bread.

'Thank you; I like it.' No, that was wrong, it sounded defiant and she didn't mean that. She added in a much softer voice, 'I'm glad you like it.'

He ate then and she put dirty dishes on her tray. Then he said, 'When're you going to Italy with me?'

She laughed. 'I got some previous engagements before. Any other time, though.'

'I'm told it's nice there,' said Holton and she noticed that he looked sad and she was happy to think that he was a little concerned about her, that he was almost serious when he talked about Italy.

'Maybe we'll go some other time,' she said.

'Sure,' said Holton, 'maybe we'll go some other time.' He drank his coffee. He looked at his watch. 'Lord, I'm late,' he said. He paid her quickly. 'See you at lunch.'

'See you at lunch, Mr Holton.' She watched him go out the door and into the crowded street.

She cleared his table. Then she went gaily back to the kitchen, her hair bobbing mysteriously in its snood. She was glad she hadn't told him she'd seen him in Times Square.

'Late aren't you?' asked Caroline when Holton came into the office. She knew he was late but she was in a mood of violent humour; she was always this way when she was happy and she was happy today because of Trebling.

'Not very,' said Holton and he went to his desk. Mr Murphy hadn't come in yet and he was safe. Caroline sat for a moment enjoying the pale white sunlight that shone across her desk. Then she got up and came over to Holton's desk.

She was awkward now. She wanted to find out things but she didn't want to be subtle. She tried anyway. 'I was out with Jim last night,' she began.

'How do you like him?' Holton wasn't paying much attention to her and this was irritating. He was busy putting books on his desk. She looked around to see if anyone was watching. Kuppelton was out of the room and no one else appeared interested. She sat down on his desk.

'I like him quite a bit,' she said.

He looked at her. 'Good,' he said. 'Jim's a fine fellow. You'll have fun playing around with him.'

'I suppose I will.'

'Just don't take him too seriously, though. He's sort of an expert with girls.' How shallow Holton was, thought Caroline. 'Just play with him and you'll be all right. A lot of girls've liked him.'

'I can understand that. He's really serious about starting something himself. At least he doesn't want to work for somebody like everybody else wants.' She wanted this to be sharp; she didn't care if it hurt or not.

167

'That's a good thing to want,' said Holton. How dull he is, thought Caroline, comparing him unfavourably with Jim Trebling.

There was nothing she wanted to know from Holton. 'How was your society party?' she asked.

'It was O.K.,' said Holton. 'It was interesting.'

'I'll bet,' thought Caroline. She was impatient of others now that she knew she was appreciated, knew that she was to see Trebling that night. 'Well, don't work too hard,' said Caroline, getting up from the desk. 'By the way, I'm going out with Jim tonight.'

'Better be careful,' said Holton seriously.

She laughed. 'I'm always careful; didn't you know that?'

Heywood was feeling well. He had managed to get home early the night before. That was one advantage in going to the theatre alone : you didn't have to go some place afterwards and get drunk.

He sat contentedly in the mahogany twilight of his large office, looking at a photograph of himself. There was no particular work to be done. Golden hadn't bothered him yet and it would be almost an hour before he had his first conference.

A buzz came out of the box on his desk. He pressed a button.

'Mr Murphy to see you,' said his secretary, concealed in the box.

'Send him in.' There was something he had to tell Murphy. Something to do with the party. The young man, Robert Holton : he was to do something for him.

'Good morning, Murphy.' Mr Heywood did not bother to rise.

'Morning, Mr Heywood,' said Murphy and Heywood wished his voice wasn't so loud. It jarred the twilight mood of the office.

'I've got some statistics here, the ones on Steel stocks; the ones showing fluctuation and . . .'

'Ah, yes, Murphy, that's very good of you to have them for me so promptly. I have another matter to discuss . . .' Heywood paused to make sure that Murphy was listening to him carefully. 'This boy, Holton,' he went on, 'I think he might do better dealing with the public, don't you?'

'Yes,' said Murphy judiciously, 'yes, I think that might be a good place for him. You saw him last night?'

'What? Oh, yes, I saw him last night. I had a pleasant talk with him. He's a clever young man, I think.'

'Yes, he's got a good head on his shoulders,' agreed Murphy.

'You will tell him, won't you, about his promotion and, ah, transfer?'

'Certainly. He'll be glad to hear this. I'll be glad to tell him. And, by the way, there's another matter in my section . . .'

'And what is that?' asked Heywood gently, trying not to yawn.

'Well, we've a man named Kuppelton who's always done a good job and I think he should get the usual promotion in that department. The one we had in mind for Holton.'

Heywood sighed. 'Certainly, Murphy; I rely, as always, on your recommendation in these cases.'

'Thank you . . .' They talked then of nothing that interested Mr Heywood. Finally Murphy left.

Mr Heywood yawned and stretched. He was rested and almost happy. He would make good decisions today. He sat back in his chair and looked at the photograph of himself. He would divorce his wife and go to South America for a year. Or perhaps he wouldn't divorce his wife but take her to South America instead. It was strange but he looked younger now than he did when the photograph was taken several years before.

When Kuppelton heard the news his first impulse was to call his mother immediately on the phone and tell her all about it. He decided not to, though, because, after all, it wasn't completely official. He did talk to Holton about it.

'Congratulations,' he said as he came over to Holton's desk. Mr Murphy had already gone to lunch and it was safe to talk.

'Thanks,' said Holton, smiling. He didn't seem as happy as Kuppelton expected him to be.

'Caroline just told me that Mr Murphy told you you were going to be a customers' man and I'm certainly glad to see you're getting ahead. I always thought that this job would be too small to hold you.' He paused. 'When do you think you'll move out?' he asked, looking away.

'The first of next week probably.' Holton chuckled. 'I guess you'll be sorry to see me leave.'

Kuppelton recognized the sarcasm but he didn't care. 'Sure I'm sorry. Of course, it's good news, in a way, for me.'

'It is at that.'

'You sure got a good deal. Well, you can't beat City Hall I always say.'

'You always say that?'

'What? Well, no, but . . . What I meant was . . .'

Robert Holton only laughed.

Kuppelton tried to talk some more with him but it was very difficult; they never had liked each other, anyway. Kuppelton left him to go to lunch.

He was jubilant but dignified as he put on his coat and hat and walked down the corridor. He would have a lot of news to tell his mother tonight. Everything had worked out nicely and soon he would be making more money and everyone he knew was happy.